Enjoy!

Jackie Shemwell

April 2016

The Devil in
Canaan Parish

JACKIE SHEMWELL

DEDICATION

This, my first novel, is lovingly dedicated to my husband, D. Wade, my sons Zach and Josh, and everyone who has ever encouraged, supported and believed in me. Most importantly, I thank God, who has kept me in his loving hands and always keeps his amazing promises.

CONTENTS

ACKNOWLEDGMENTS

So much gratitude goes into this book. In addition to God, I want to thank my parents, Chris Smith and Glen Burns; my family and friends, especially those who read early drafts and encouraged me – Alana and Patrick Placzkowski, Samantha Yang, Rebecca Jenshak, Debby Hill, Nathaniel Means, Tucker Smathers, Lester McNeely, Betty Gaillard and Ruth Switzer. Thank you also to Dylan Drake Design for your amazing talent and tremendous help with my paperback edition and my author website.

CHAPTER ONE

She looked like she had already drowned, the first time I saw her. It was something about her expression. Dead. Devoid of emotion, she stared through you like the dead do, her gaze like one's own reflection in black glassy water at the bottom of a barrel. I could not see the color of her eyes, eclipsed by her pupils, and the water seemed to pour out of her like from a corpse just pulled from the river. It fell in giant droplets from her ridiculous straw hat and ran from her long stringy hair, down her pale cheeks, and through the mottled blue fabric of her faded cotton dress. It pooled in the folds of her nylon socks, once white knee-highs, now muddy red and bunched around her ankles. She clutched a small carpetbag in front of her, her shoulders stooped forward, either from its weight, or in an attempt to shield herself from view. She gazed somewhere behind me, I thought, or perhaps her eyes saw something that was not there. She stood just inside the doorway, careful to keep herself over the floor mat where the water dripping from her small, shivering frame was forming a large puddle around her.

I did not notice the old man until he began coughing. He was standing next to her, further inside the store, his clumsy felt hat held between his fingertips in front of his chest as if it were a fragile china plate. He seemed made of mud, dressed in monochromatic brown from head to toe, the dirt of months without bathing caked in the folds of his skin from his furrowed forehead to his double chin. He was dressed in what must have been his only suit, perhaps the one he was married in, some thirty years ago from the look of it. He appeared sixty, but was most likely fifty. The life of the swamp folk was hard and unrelenting. The sound of his raspy wheezing cough made me think he would not have to endure it much longer. His enormous gut shook with the effort of breathing, and in an attempt at decorum, he pulled a dripping handkerchief out of his pocket and hacked into it.

I opened my mouth to speak and was startled when the voice that came was not my own. My father-in-law had appeared in front of me, and I could see the light reflecting off the top of his fat, balding head.

"May I help you folks? We were just about to close with the storm coming and all, but we'd be glad to stay open for a few more minutes if there's something we can get for you. Some cough syrup, maybe?"

I could tell how his face would look without even seeing it -- the eyes wide behind his gold-rimmed glasses and a practiced smile curling the edges of his lips. Salesmanship flowed through his veins. He was the third generation owner of the only drugstore in all of Canaan Parish: Bordelon's.

"No sir. We was jest, I mean, pardon me sir, I'm Mouton. Allain Mouton," said the man, in a thick Cajun accent, jamming his hat and handkerchief into his left fist and extending the fat stubby fingers of his right hand out to my father-in-law.

"Pleased to meet you, sir. I'm Charlie Bordelon. This is my son-in-law."

Mouton nodded toward me and I returned the gesture. I was not important enough to have a name.

Bordelon examined Mouton. I watched as he quietly wiped the man's moisture from his hands onto his apron, pure white and starched so stiff it hung like armor from his chest down past his knees. His impeccable shoes glistened like a shiny new coin, and he stood with his heels cemented together. Sometimes it seemed as though his spinal column were also starched, his posture was so rigid and unyielding.

"How can I help you, Mr. Mouton?"

Mouton glanced over his shoulder at the girl and cleared his throat.

"This here my daughter, Melee. She a real good cook. Real good. She good cleaning in the house, too you know. She do the laundry, she can even press and starch your shirts."

"My well, that's wonderful, Mr. Mouton. I'm sure you're very pleased with her," said Bordelon, the sweet syrup of his voice taking on just a hint of sour, a delicacy lost on the visitor. Instead he became more relaxed, breaking into a wide smile.

"Oui, bien sur, I am. But uh, you see I ain't got no more use for her, you see."

Bordelon cocked his head to one side.

"I beg your pardon?" he asked.

"Et bon, I going marry soon. You see? Her mother, you know, she been dead a long time, and now I going marry again. You see? So I uh, going have a new wife soon. And you know it no good with two women in one house."

Bordelon said nothing in return. I began to enjoy the exchange, although I kept watching the girl. At the mention of her domestic virtues, she hung her head and began staring instead at the muddy tips of her dilapidated Mary Janes.

"So, you see," Mouton continued, "I need to find a new place for her, and I come here." He ended with a nod and a slight bow, relieved that his long-prepared speech was finally delivered.

"Well, uh, Mr. Mouton," my father-in-law began, "I appreciate you bringing your daughter, but we really have no openings here in the store. We have all the staff we need at this time."

"Mais non, mais non!" said Mouton. "No I mean, not here. Not for the store. She don't know nothing about shops and such. I mean, I heard you was looking for a hired girl."

"Me? I'm not sure where you got that from." Bordelon was shaking his head, his brow furrowed and lips pursed.

"Perhaps he means me. That is to say, perhaps he means Sally." I spoke up.

My wife Sally was Bordelon's first and favorite daughter of three. We had been married for almost ten years, and had been through twice as many maids. The most recent one lasted two weeks before she ran out of the house in tears after my wife threw a frying pan across the kitchen, shouting that the girl's cooking was inedible.

"What?" said Bordelon, turning his head and removing his glasses. He was unused to the spontaneous sound of my voice.

"Sally. She wants a new girl. The last one didn't work out. I guess she's been telling the women at Church and the Ladies Auxiliary. I'm sure word must have gotten around by now."

Bordelon turned away from the visitors' view and squinted his eyes at me. I knew I had said something that displeased him.

"Mr. Mouton, will you excuse me and my son-in-law? We'll be right back with you." He motioned me toward the back of the store, and I turned and went with him close on my heels down the narrow aisle filled with salves, ointments, bandages, syrups, and gauze. When we got to the lunch counter, I turned and waited for him to speak.

"Palmer, what the hell is going on over in your house? That was the third girl my wife sent over to you in four months."

"I know sir." I said. "It's Sally. She's just . . real particular.

"Mmm hmm." He said, eyeing me up. I said nothing more, accepting my fate. No matter what was going on or how badly Sally behaved, it was always going to be my fault.

"Palmer, I don't know about this girl," he said. "I don't think my Sally wants any coon-ass in her kitchen. Why don't you get another nice clean colored girl?"

"Sir, I don't think there are any nice clean colored girls left in Louisiana who haven't already worked in our home. Maybe a white girl would do better."

"White trash, more like." he said. "But, I guess it's not my place to decide this. You should tell her to come round tomorrow and have Sally look her over."

I swallowed back the desire to laugh. When had anything not been 'his place' to decide? 'Daddy' was still Lord and Master to Sally, and I felt his dominion even under my own roof. But, the social theater of south Louisiana was founded on "knowing one's place." From the wealthy white descendants of plantation owners, to the poor black sons of slaves, creoles from the black islands of the Caribbean, to the Cajun swamp folk who scratched a living from fishing and hunting, those outcasts from Acadia, all of us played a particular role on life's grand stage and there was no room for extemporization. One missed cue, one slipped line, and the entire production would be cast into chaos.

"That's probably a good idea," I said. "But I'd hate to send her back home this evening. I mean, they probably walked all day to get here, and that storm is going to be fierce." I wasn't sure why I was contesting him -- perhaps only because I had the slightest chance to do so, which never happened.

He cocked his head to the side again, as if thinking of a retort, another reason why I shouldn't take her home with me, another reason why he was right and I was wrong, but at that moment a great thunderclap broke overhead, rattling the shelves and causing some of the medicine bottles to clink together.

"Aw hell," he said waving his hand at me. "I don't care what you do. If Sally don't like her I guess that's your problem." He turned and walked back to his office to finish up the day's accounts, slamming the door on our conversation.

A thrill went through me. I was giddy that in some small way I had won. For the first time in years I wasn't irritated that my father-in-law did not trust me to do the accounting. Every morning he counted out the cash drawers and every evening he locked himself in his office to go over the receipts. He would question me over a penny, squinting up sideways at me through those gold-rimmed glasses, perched at the end of his nose. Tonight, as every night, I was free to go as soon as I'd swept the floor and locked up, and tonight I was actually glad to be going home.

I walked back to the front of the store where Mouton was twirling a display of postcards near the door. He straightened up when he saw me coming, holding his hat in front of him again, in silent supplication. The girl had not moved, but the puddle around her had grown quite large and the dripping had nearly stopped.

"Mr. Mouton, I'd like to take uh, Melee to my home tonight to meet my wife, Sally. I think that she'll be pleased to see her. We've been without a maid for a few weeks now and my wife has been quite anxious about it." I said, speaking to him, but watching the girl, who was still studying her shoes.

"Melee, you hear dat? C'est bon, n'est pas?" Mouton asked his daughter. She glanced up at him and nodded, then turned her head toward me.

I stifled a gasp when I saw her face, this time tilted up into the light. Her eyes were the color of Spanish moss, deep-set, with indigo circles under them. Her nose, like the rest of her slight frame, was thin, which made her high cheekbones even more pronounced. Her heart-shaped face ended in a tiny, bony chin, but it was her lips that surprised me: deep red and succulent, they reminded me of ripe plums, plump and ready for picking. The lower lip was jutted out in a slight pout. She raised her dark lashes, still wet from the rain, and peered at me through them. The effect was devastating. I felt my knees begin to buckle, and I reached into my pocket to grab my handkerchief and wipe the moisture from my upper lip.

"Miss Mouton," I said. "I'm Bram Palmer. Would you like to come to my house to meet my wife?"

"It's Melee," she whispered.

Her father turned toward her. I saw the muscles in his fist flex and the slightest flinch of her shoulders away from him. I realized that he was exerting an enormous effort to restrain himself from cuffing her, and the dejected way she hung her head made me know that she was used to it.

"Oh, yes, of course, Melee, would you like to come?" I asked, trying to collect myself.

"Yes sir," she answered.

"And you're old enough, right?" I said, suddenly remembering to ask.

"Yes sir, I'm eighteen."

"And you've been a maid before?"

"No, sir," she shook her head.

"Now, dat don't mean nothing do it?" Mouton asked, anxiously. He stepped slightly forward into my line of sight.

"It would be preferable," I replied. "But if she's a good worker, and respectful, I think she'll be fine."

Mouton sighed. "C'est bon, c'est bon! Tank you, Mr. Palmer," he said, extending his hand to me.

I shook it and nodded. "Not at all."

"You take good care of my Melee, now," he forced a smiled.

"Of course," I assured him, turning again toward the girl. She was staring through me again, at that spot somewhere behind my head and beyond the store itself. There was no indication of any emotion from her about the news that she would be coming with me to my home, perhaps to work for my wife and I for quite some time. She seemed indifferent to her fate.

"Adieu, Melee," said Mouton. He leaned forward to attempt to embrace her, and she turned her cheek toward him. He gave it a quick peck, and then replaced the hat on his head.

"Adieu, Papa," she murmured, not moving her eyes from that far-away spot.

Mouton turned with a grunt, and hurried out the door, perhaps afraid I would change my mind. The cowbell hung from the door-handle made a noisy clang after his departure. I followed behind him, removing the key from around my neck, and locking the door. As I peered through the glass, I saw no sign of him. The dark slanting rain had already swallowed him up. I flipped the "Yes, We're Open!" sign over to "Sorry, We're Closed", and then turned back to the silent figure beside me.

"So, I'll just collect my things, and then we'll go, alright?" I announced, not sure why I felt the need to ask her permission. She nodded, still not stirring from her strange trance.

"Follow me."

She floated behind me down the aisle and waited next to the lunch counter as I removed my apron and hung it up. I grabbed my raincoat and hat from the coat rack and put them on. Then I went to the light switch and shut them all down. The only light in the building now shone through the crack around the office door where I knew my father-in-law would be staying for at least another hour, finishing up the day's receipts.

"Good night then, sir," I called. I heard him mumble something in reply.

I opened the back door and held it wide, beckoning for Melee to come. Awoken from her reverie, she stiffened her shoulders and walked toward me. The rain was pounding outside, spraying my face through the open doorway. I had my umbrella with me, and I opened it, while holding the door open with my elbow. I didn't need to direct her. She joined me under the umbrella, and I turned and slammed the heavy door.

My car was a few short paces away in the parking lot, a 1948 metallic green Buick Roadmaster. Bordelon had given it to my wife as a wedding gift. It was brand-new then, top of the line.

"Nothing but the best for my Sally," Bordelon had crowed.

He gave her the keys at our reception, and she shrieked and ran outside in her wedding dress to see it. She was crying and hugging him around the neck, over and over, as all our guests came outside and gathered around to admire it. For the rest of the reception Bordelon strutted from table to table, high on the congratulations he was receiving. It was one of the most ostentatious displays the town had seen since before the Great Depression. It was a sign that better days were ahead.

The car was also a means for my father-in-law to briefly escape from the shadow of his father-in-law. The Bordelons were not wealthy. The drugstore had provided them with a comfortable living, but they still had to work for it. Charlie Bordelon's real money came from his wife, Alice Landry. The Landrys had a large sugar cane plantation and owned much of the land around Techeville before the civil war. This land had been sold off over time, and the family plantation was now producing only a token amount of sugar, but the Landrys still lived there in the Grande Maison. Mr. and Mrs. Landry, my wife's grandparents, were Lord and Lady of the tiny kingdom of Techeville in Canaan Parish, Louisiana. My father-in-law may have given us the car, but it was Old Man Landry who slipped the deed to our house into my dress coat pocket as he was leaving the reception hall, something he would do for all sixteen of his married grandchildren.

Ironically, Sally did not know how to drive and never learned, thus the car became mine by default. I opened the passenger side door and held it for Melee. She looked awkward in the front seat, as though she wasn't quite sure how to ride in an automobile, and her shaking hands pulled the hem of her skirt down over her legs and then folded in her lap. Grabbing her bag from her hand, I tossed it into the back seat.

I walked around to the driver's side door and slid inside. I was dripping wet, but the heat of the July evening kept me from feeling chilled. Rain in South Louisiana was warmed by the heat of the Gulf. It never refreshed you. It felt more like jumping into a hot bath on a summer day. It made you drowsy and weak, and it fell hard, pounding the muscles in your arms, your back, your legs, pummeling the top of your head until you gave up trying to shield yourself and just let the abuse come. It was hurricane season, and so the rain was slamming down sideways, propelled by the high winds of a tropical depression.

I started the car, and cursed under my breath at the immediacy with which the front windows fogged up. It would be difficult to see my way home. I turned on the lights and the windshield wipers and backed out of the parking lot. Pulling into the town square, I drove around the courthouse and then proceeded up the road to my house. My car could have driven itself. It was a ten-minute drive at most, and I had done it every morning, noon and evening for the last ten years. That thought, and the fact that no one would be braving the storm, made me fairly confident I could make it home without crashing the car. As we drove north out of town, the First Baptist Church with its massive neoclassical columns and white painted steeple, towered over my left. To my right loomed the levee, keeping the Bayou Teche in check.

The bayou was given its name by the Indians who lived in this area long ago. The legend was that a giant snake wound through the lands and attacked their villages. The warriors finally killed the snake and its carcass rotted where it lay. The depression it left became the bayou, and now the levee systems protected the good townspeople of Techeville from its bite. Further south, there was a bridge and the road to New Orleans. Beyond that, the levees ceased and the bayou continued wild and free, leaving the poor blacks in the Bottoms and the Cajuns in the marsh lands to fend for themselves against it.

The pounding rain and the constant swish of the windshield wipers lulled me into a kind of trance that was unbroken until I pulled into the long drive next to our home. The drive went around behind the house and ended at the garage. I leapt out of the car and ran to yank the garage door open as the rain pounded my face and hands. Then I returned to the car and pulled it into the garage. The sound of the rain died away as I turned off the ignition, leaving my passenger and myself in relative quiet. For a moment, I heard only the sound of the blood rushing in my ears from my recent exertion, and then I could hear the slow in and out of Melee's breath. From the corner of my eye I discerned the outline of her nipples beneath her soaked dress. I had not noticed them at the store, but sitting in the car caused the fabric to pull tight across her chest. I found myself turning toward her, watching the up and down pattern of her breasts as her lungs filled and emptied of air. I was surprised by the sudden tug I felt in the crotch of my pants, and I quickly cleared my throat to break the silence.

"Are you ready to go in?" I asked.

She turned to me and nodded. The garage was small. Not big enough for me to go around the side and open the door for her. I pulled her bag from the back seat, stepped out, and then reached my hand in.

"I'm sorry, but you'll have to slide your way out," I said.

She gathered her skirt up and reached for my hand. The delicate fingers were rough and strong, and she held my palm in a firm grip. The touch sent an electric current through me, and I struggled to compose my face muscles after she emerged from the car. I had to reach around her to close the door, and at that moment, my chest brushed against her back, and I could feel her muscles tense. I turned to look at her and she gazed up at me, waiting for my next direction. I froze for a moment, suddenly wishing I had taken a longer way home and engaged in some small talk in the car, but at that moment I heard the screeching of the kitchen screen's door in the back of the house and knew that my wife was waiting for us inside.

CHAPTER TWO

The house that Sally and I lived in was built in the Acadian style. The whole structure was elevated four feet off the ground on brick columns. The high, sloped roof formed two large porches that ran along the front and back of the house. From the front door, one-stepped into a large gallery with a dining room on the right and parlor on the left. These two rooms had French doors opening onto the porch, allowing for ample space to entertain guests who could mill about from dining room to gallery to parlor, out the doors to the porch and back in again.

The back of the house held the bathroom and master bedroom to the left, and a large, eat-in kitchen to the right. A swinging door connected the dining room to the kitchen. The bedroom had another set of French doors opening to a private, screened-in porch in back. The kitchen's screen door also opened onto the back porch, but the two areas were separated by a half wall.

There were no other bedrooms in the house. Upstairs, a long, open attic with windows on either side of the house was where we kept our storage and also a makeshift room for our maids. This was called the garconniere and was reached by a narrow staircase from the kitchen. Ten years ago, my wife and I had planned to partition off this space to make additional rooms for the children. Through the course of our marriage it became evident that this would not be necessary. Sally had been unable to have children.

As I walked with Melee under the umbrella toward the back steps, I could see my wife sitting at the kitchen table, reading the paper and smoking a cigarette. I could tell by her posture that she was trying to appear nonchalant, but I also knew that she had just opened the kitchen door to check why it was taking me so long to come into the house. Her blond hair was neatly coiffed and her long painted nails and lipstick matched the large red strawberries that decorated the white cotton dress she wore. It was hard to tell she was only 33 years old. She had aged so drastically since the day I first saw her at a Catholic college in New Orleans.

When I met Sally, I was a soldier fresh from the war and not sure what to do with myself. My father had been a traveling salesman of religious artifacts: bibles, crucifixes, rosaries, statues of the Virgin Mary and St. Francis, St. Christopher charms, and the like. I spent my childhood living in greasy run-down motels, boarding houses and the backseat of the family car. We traveled back and forth across the southern coast. Through Galveston, Biloxi, Mobile, Panama City, and Jacksonville my father went door to door or set up camp outside of church revivals. We spent the hurricane season mostly in Savannah, but my father always wanted to be back in New Orleans by Mardi Gras and the Lenten season. New Orleans was a mecca for my father's wares. From Catholic nuns to Voodoo priestesses, the demand was great, and my father would sometimes set up a stand in Jackson square. These times were always the happiest for me, because we'd have enough money to get a small apartment where my mother could cook us cornbread and red beans, and I could go to a real school.

On my eighteenth birthday, I enlisted in the army. It was November, and we were in Savannah. That morning I said goodbye to my mother and father and headed straight to the recruitment office. One month later, Japan attacked Pearl Harbor and by early spring, when I knew my parents would be settling down in New Orleans, I was in the Philippines. There was no way for me to write to them. They had no permanent address, and so I spent the years in Japanese prison camps wondering where they were and if I'd ever see them again. I was discharged in January 1946, and I headed to New Orleans to wait for Mardi Gras and hope that I might find the old man's stand somewhere in Jackson square. I never did.

I spent the next six months getting as drunk as I could. When I ran out of money, a prostitute I was frequenting kicked me out of her apartment in the French Quarter. That morning, I took my last nickel and hopped on the streetcar to the garden district, determined to go as far as that nickel would take me. I got off across the street from the college. This seemed like a sign to a naïve 23-year-old, so I walked up to the admissions office and announced I wanted to use my GI Bill money to enroll.

I decided to study poetry, because I liked some of what I had read during my brief time in high school. I found myself in a class full of women and was surprised to be somewhat of a novelty. Most men my age were either dead, in a hospital, or married to the sweethearts they had left behind before the war. The girls fawned over me and it wasn't long before I was having all the free sex I wanted. I soon realized, however, that I was not cut out for literature and my grades began failing. A girl who had not slipped me her number, in fact had never really spoken to me, impressed me in class. She kept to herself, but she was often called on by the professor and always had a thoughtful answer. One day I approached her to ask if she could tutor me.

Her name was Sally Bordelon, and after weeks of begging, I convinced her I wasn't a predator. We began to meet in the school library where we would spend hours reading Keats, Shelley and Byron. Sally was also quite adept in French and spent time translating Baudelaire for me. She would read passages to me and try to hide her mirth at my preposterous interpretations. I was lured by her genteel expressions. She came from a family with money, and I had never been with anyone of her league. She wasn't arrogant, just quiet and reserved, and I used to try my best to crack through the careful exterior and make her laugh. It wasn't often, but when she did laugh it rang through the library like silver bells. She would clap her pretty hand over her mouth and shake her platinum curls at me.

It was not long before we were steady sweethearts. I would take her to the picture show, and out to dinner and on long walks along the river. Sometimes she would let me kiss her before she ran inside her dorm, and sometimes a little more, but always she was a good Catholic girl, and I think the fact that I couldn't have her made me want her. She graduated in the spring and went back home to Techeville where I thought she would forget about me. I wrote her a few letters, doing my best imitation of the Romantic poets she so idolized, expecting to never get a reply.

But the replies came, frequent and fervent. It was as though the passion she could not show me in person was unleashed on the page. She signed her letters "your Madeline," and would finish them with a line from *The Eve of St. Agnes:*

> *Give me that voice again, my Porphyro,*
> *Those looks immortal, those complainings dear!*
> *Oh leave me not in this eternal woe,*
> *For if thou diest, my Love, I know not where to go.*

I did my best to match her letters' ardor in my own, calling her "my heaven" and proclaiming the aching of my soul, but it didn't seem to matter. Her love for me was complete, and I had only to claim her if I still wanted her. She begged me to spend my Christmas break with her and her family, and having nowhere else to go, I obliged.

I was dazzled. I did not understand from what kind of money Sally came until I visited her family's little kingdom in Canaan Parish. The parties were sumptuous and elegant and lasted until the early morning hours. The women dressed in opulent silk gowns and the men wore white tie tuxedos. Smartly dressed servants circled the room bearing silver trays and an endless supply of champagne and hors d'oeuvres. Sally became an enchanting princess on my arm. She was witty and charming and beautiful. I was astonished to see this side of her, and I relished being the one man in the room who had her full attention. She was again my tutor, this time in the art of sparkling conversation and social etiquette and delighted in providing me entrée into her world of power and prestige, a world I had only ever read about.

Caught up in the heady pageantry and intoxicating brilliance of Christmas Eve, I asked her father's permission for her hand in marriage. He squinted his eyes at me and wrinkled up his nose the way he did when he sniffed an ancient bottle of cough syrup at his drugstore to see if it was still good enough to sell.

"Palmer," he said. "That ain't no Jew name, is it?"

"No sir. Scottish, I think."

"Well, I guess I'd better say yes, then," he said. "Seems like Sally's got it in her head that you're the man for her, although damned if I can see why." He then took a sip of his brandy and nodded to me, to indicate the conversation was over.

I soon learned that whatever Sally wanted, Sally got, and Sally had sets her sights on me, the noble savage of her dreams. My nomadic existence as a loner and outsider made me the forbidden fruit, the Porphyro come to storm the castle and whisk the sheltered virgin away to a life of excitement and mystery.

On Christmas day we were having dinner at the Grande Maison on her grandparents' plantation. The entire Landry family was there – Sally's mother was one of five siblings – and the majestic old house was filled with laughter, rambunctious children, music, drink and dancing. During a quiet moment, I pulled Sally out to the porch, got down on my knee and offered her the tiny diamond I had in my pocket, a ring I had purchased on credit at the jewelry store in Techeville. Overjoyed, she shrieked, and then grabbed my hand and ran with me into the house. I had intended to make the announcement myself at dinner, but an impulsive Sally made it for me. She ran from room to room, shouting the news and kissing the well-wishers. I followed her, red-faced and smiling, trying to remember the names of everyone I was meeting. I was again surprised to see the passionate side of quiet, demure Sally. It was almost as if there were two of her.

The following spring we were married. I had agreed to convert to Catholicism -- it seemed as good a religion as any -- so that she could have her lavish wedding at the Catholic church in town. The church was crammed with family and friends – Sally Landry Bordelon's wedding was the social event of the year. There was no one from my side of the family coming, and so Sally's family filled that half of the church too.

Through the generosity of our wedding guests, we started our marriage with a car and a house filled with the finest china, crystal, cutlery furnishings and linens money could buy. We spent our honeymoon on Grand Isle, and returned to Techeville where Sally wanted to set up housekeeping.

Faced with the sudden realization that I needed to begin earning a living to support the two of us, I told Sally that I wanted to go back to college to complete my degree, but she wouldn't have it. The night we discussed it, she burst into tears and took to her bed with a migraine. It was the first of hundreds of migraines she would have in years to come. At the time, I was a newlywed and disturbed by my wife's sudden incapacitation. I called her parents, who rushed to her bedside. I told them what I thought had caused the attack, and her father ushered me outside. There on the porch over a cigarette, he offered me the position at the drugstore. He told me that if I quit school, he would guarantee Sally and me a comfortable living for the rest of our days. He said that since he had no sons, the drugstore would go to me after his death, and then I could in turn pass it on to our children. Not wanting to turn down such a generous offer, and not having any real prospects of my own, I agreed.

For a while after that my wife and I were happy. I worked at the drugstore, learning the business, and Sally played housewife. Her cooking was abominable, but I managed to choke through the sawdust she served me. Eighteen months of pent-up frustration made our lovemaking passionate and frequent at first. She was willing and enthusiastic, but also modest and shy. It was time when the two sides of Sally struggled most against each other. The shutters had to be closed, the door had to be locked and the lights had to be out. There was no question of us being intimate anywhere other than in our bedroom, in our marriage bed. Still, she was capable of long hours of insatiable desire, and it was a happy time for us.

Soon, however, there was a subtle shift in Sally's demeanor. She became anxious and petulant. It had been nearly a year since our wedding, and she was still not pregnant. The edges of her mouth were more often turned down than up, and I noticed a furrowing of her brow. At work, my father-in-law engaged me in the first of many, many meddling conversations about my marriage.

"You know, Palmer," he said one day, "I think Sally may be a little too overworked."

I was stocking one of the aisles, putting green bottles of insect bite medicine in a straight line with the labels facing outward. The store was empty and silent, and I was startled by my father-in-law's sudden statement. Usually the man never spoke to me, except to tell me to ring up a customer or direct me to get another box of inventory.

"Sorry, sir?" I stammered, not sure if I had heard him.

"Well, it's Sally, you know. She's not used to running a household by herself. You know my wife talks to her quite a bit and she told me that Sally seems overwrought. She's got too much to do."

I wasn't sure what he meant. Our house was small, we had a maid that came to clean once a week, we had a boy to take care of the yard and the garden, all that Sally had really to occupy her time was preparing meals and doing laundry, which wasn't much with just the two of us.

"It's. . .it's just too much for her," he continued. "I think it might be best if you get a house girl. Someone permanent, to take care of all the cooking and cleaning and what-not."

"Oh," I said, beginning to understand, "Sir, I don't think that would be necessary, I mean I think we're alright, just the two of us."

"Palmer, I want to have grandchildren before I'm old, alright?" he said.

Again, I was confused, not sure what he could mean. I could tell he was getting exasperated with me.

"Sally can't concentrate on having babies when she's wearing herself out around the house. Now it's all settled. I'm paying for you to have a live-in maid, and my wife is going to send one over for you," with that, he turned on his heels and marched back to his office.

I was too shocked to answer. That evening I went home and, sure enough, dinner was being prepared by the first of a long line of domestic help. This one's name was Ruby. She was in her forties and had worked for both the Landrys and the Bordelons. She was an excellent cook, housekeeper, and laundress, and for a while Sally was happy again. She began to walk around the house singing lullabies. I would come home to find her relaxing on the back porch in our little sitting area, reading a book or working a crossword puzzle. We continued trying for a baby, and spent a joyful summer together. By the beginning of autumn, Sally was pregnant.

We decided to announce the good news at the annual Landry Christmas party and once again, Sally ran from room to room laughing and kissing everyone. Old man Landry proposed a toast to us over the dinner table, and the whole family applauded. My father-in-law was pleasant to me, patting me on the back and inviting me to join the men in the parlor for some brandy, cigars and poker. I obliged, eager and excited to finally be part of the inner circle.

The months went by, and Sally and I continued in marital bliss. Mardi Gras came, and we spent the evening watching the parades, celebrating until late into the night, my arm around her shoulders and one resting on her growing belly. Family and friends threw beads from the floats directly at the two of us. I would wrap each one around Sally's neck and kiss her lips. I had never seen her so happy or so beautiful.

On the morning of Ash Wednesday, Sally and I awoke, covered in blood. The sheets were soaked through with the loss of her pregnancy. When Sally realized what was happening, she collapsed in hysterics. I pulled her up out of bed, carrying her in my arms to the tub where I stripped her down and began rinsing off the blood. I yelled for Ruby, who came running in, frightened and panicked. She stifled a scream when she saw our bed. I told her to go and get the doctor and then to find the Bordelons. By the time I had wrapped a robe around Sally and was carrying her back to our bed, Ruby had returned with Doctor Collins.

The doctor went straight to our bedroom, calling for Ruby to help him. When Sally's parents arrived, her mother went to her bedside, and I paced back and forth outside the door where her father waited. I was irritated to have been banned from the room.

"Palmer," said my father-in-law, "you might want to clean yourself up."

I looked down and realized I was still in my pajamas, soaked in blood and water from washing Sally. I went into the bathroom to change. When I returned, Dr. Collins was murmuring something to my father-in-law. He straightened up when he saw me and said that Sally would be fine, but that she'd lost a lot of blood and needed absolute rest. I agreed.

"Bram, there's something else," said the doctor, hesitating.

I was confused. He glanced at Sally's father, who abruptly excused himself. After Bordelon had gone into the bedroom and shut the door, the doctor turned back to me, closed his eyes, and then heaved a sigh.

"There was a . . .baby, Bram. I had to deliver it just now. Ruby has it."

"A . . .a baby?" I stuttered. I felt as though I had been punched in the stomach.

"Well, not viable, I mean, there won't be any kind of birth or death certificate, Bram, but I am not sure how you want to. . .dispose of it."

I cringed at the words.

"Alright," I mumbled, "thank you, Doctor Collins."

I found Ruby in the kitchen, clutching something to her chest in a bloody towel. She was seated in a chair near the back door, humming and rocking back and forth. I placed my hand on her shoulder, and when she raised her head up to me, there were tears in her eyes.

"It's such a shame," she whispered. "Folks say you cain't have a soul till you're really born, but I don't believe that. Seem like something this precious has to have one too."

"Thank you, Ruby," I answered, holding my hands out.

I took just one look at my child, a girl no bigger than my hand, and then wrapped her back in the towel. I took her to the town's only funeral parlor where the director brought out a small pine box with grim courtesy.
She was buried that day, in a plot near the Landry family. The marker simply said: Palmer, d. 1950.

Over the next weeks, Sally did not leave her room. Ruby waited on her day and night, patient and kind, but Sally grew more and more annoyed by her. She could not abide that Ruby knew. One day I came home and found Ruby sitting on the front porch, her hat and gloves on, her one bag packed and sitting next to her.

"Mr. Bram," she said. "Mr. Bram, I'm sorry but I just cain't stay here no longer. Miss Sally just ain't happy with me and there ain't nothing I can do."

I tried to change her mind, but the attempt was half-hearted. I knew she was right. Sally would not be comforted until Ruby was gone.

Once Ruby left, I began to manage Sally myself -- feeding her, bathing her and dressing her. She was still very depressed, but she began to spend a little time each day sitting on the back porch and staring into the yard. Soon she was up and about again, and one day I came home to find her digging a garden.

"I'm planting a rose garden," she said when I asked. "There's not much to look at out that back porch. If I'm going to spend my time sitting there, I want something to look at."

Over the next few months she transformed the plot of yard behind the house into an impressive rose garden. This was difficult, as the heat and humidity of southern Louisiana tends to encourage black spot and mildew. As the years went by, she added more varieties, some with beautiful names like Madame Antoine Mari and La Marne. Her favorites were the Souvenir de St. Anne, a white rose with the palest hint of pink, like the blush on the cheeks of a porcelain doll. Sally told me that Saint Anne was the mother of the Virgin Mary, a barren woman whose endless prayers for a child were finally answered. She became the patron saint of my wife who, if she wasn't out in her rose garden, was in church, attending mass and praying for the child that never came.

There were no more miscarriages. There was nothing. As time moved on, there was only the drugstore, the rose garden, mass on Sunday, the annual Christmas party at the Landry mansion and all the endless social affairs in between: birthdays, cotillions, engagement parties, weddings, anniversaries, funerals. There were also the endless trips to the doctors in Lafayette and the specialists in New Orleans -- all of them unable to tell us why Sally could not get pregnant, or give hope that it would change. Dr. Collins would receive the reports from them, and he and his wife would shoot sad eyes at us across the aisle at church on Sundays.

Sally's younger sisters were married and soon had children of their own. No one asked any more if we were expecting, or when we might be. My wife's friends began to hide their pregnancies from her as long as possible, and would avoid inviting her to baby showers out of pity. Even my father-in-law ceased to bring it up, although he continued to insist his daughter had a maid, and would send over a new one, each time my wife's patience with the old one wore thin.

Time also brought distance between us. As the years rolled by, my wife became more and more like the roses she tended: delicate, beautiful, and painful to touch. I could not go near her any more unless it was our monthly attempt to produce offspring. It was done mechanically, with no joy or anticipation. She would lie there cold and stony, reminding me of the Virgin Mary statues my father used to sell. I would do my duty only because if I didn't she would tell her mother, who would tell my father-in-law, who would call me into his office yet again and scold me for my failed manhood. It would take me hours of heavy drinking before I could steel my nerves to the task, and when it was finished, she would push me off of her, disgusted by the stench of my breath.

Time passed in this manner for several years. I did my best not to upset Sally and be the cause of the terrible migraines that would inevitably come. There was nothing I could do to comfort her. For whatever reason, I could not give her the one thing that she wanted, and so nothing I gave her mattered. Like her father before me, I allowed her to make all the decisions, to have everything as she wished, and never to put forward an independent opinion that I thought she wouldn't agree with, which was why as I walked up the back steps with Melee holding my arm and sharing my umbrella, I began to panic at what Sally might say about this surprise visitor I had decided to bring to our home.

CHAPTER THREE

I reached the top of the steps and shook off the rain under the shelter of the porch. I took my soaked hat and coat and threw them on a rocking chair near the door and placed my umbrella open on its side to give it a chance to dry. I put Melee's bag down and turned toward her. She had not moved or made any effort to dry off. It was as if she wasn't sure if she needed to bother. As if she wasn't sure if she'd actually be staying or would have to go back out into that dark pounding rain.

"Wait here," I whispered, with what I hoped would be a reassuring smile, but was probably more of a grimace. I was not eager to have the conversation I was about to have with my wife.

I opened the kitchen's screen door with care, trying to minimize the screech of its hinges, making a mental note that I needed to ask Gabriel, our yard boy, to oil them. Sally was still sitting at the table, reading the newspaper spread out in front of her, the long ash of her lit cigarette dangling where she held it in her right hand. She didn't look up at me.

"Honey, I've brought someone here to meet you. Someone to help us out a bit," I said, thinking it best to cut through the pleasantries and just be out with it.

"I know," said Sally curtly. She clipped the end of her cigarette off in the ashtray and crushed it out. "Daddy called and told me."

"Oh, he did, huh?" I said, breaking into a sweat. I should have known.

"Yes, and you needn't have bothered," snapped Sally, beginning to fold up the newspaper. "There is no way under the sun that I'm going to have a back-woods Cajun girl with no manners and no references running my house."

"Sally, honey, be fair," I pleaded. She was standing up and straightening the folds in her dress. I could tell she had been furious, waiting for me to get home so that she could send the offensive girl back where she came from.

"Bram, I mean it. I declare I don't know where you got the notion that I'd be happy with this. . .this. . .arrangement. I do have a reputation in town to uphold, whether or not I'm your wife."

The last part hurt, and I knew what she meant by it. The pure blood line of the Landry family had already been diluted by Alice Landry's marriage to a middle class shopkeeper the likes of Charlie Bordelon. Sally's marriage to me had brought down the family name even further. She could no longer call herself Sally Landry Bordelon. She was now Sally Bordelon Palmer, and it was only her constant appearance on the social circuit and reminders about "Grandma and Grandpa Landry" that kept her from being just another middle class housewife. We had no real money of our own; nothing that had not been given to us. Our membership in the local country club, the domestic help, all the trappings that kept us floating in her grandparents' social sphere were paid for by Bordelon, or more specifically by his wife Alice with the money she received from her parents. We still had the car we'd gotten for our wedding, nearly ten years old now, and no money or plans for a new one. We were still living in the same "starter" house her grandfather provided us, and I knew that we would be there for the rest of our lives. If by some miracle we ever did have children, we had no money to give them. My son would have to join me in the drug store and my daughter would not have the means to be a debutante. I could tell from the smirk on Sally's face, by the way her upper lip curled in disdain, by the anger smoldering behind the controlled tone of her voice, that she had lost all respect for me. In another time or place perhaps she would have left me, but in Canaan Parish, a good Catholic girl descended from French nobility did not get a divorce.

My usual reaction to her disappointment in me was guilt and regret that I could not make her happy or be the man that she wanted. I had always known I didn't come from good stock, and had no business being with a woman of her worth. Sometimes I thought I should never have asked her to help me with my homework that day back in college and should have known my place and stuck to it. But that evening I felt differently. Perhaps I was still buoyed by the small victory over her father I had tasted back at the drugstore and knew that I could not, would not, be able to face Bordelon in the morning only to report that he had won the war and that Sally had made me send the offensive girl back to the swamp she came from. I looked around me, trying to gain some strength and happened to hear a faint sigh behind me. It was Melee, and it was the first sign of emotion she had shown. I could tell that she understood she would not be staying and that my wife did not want her. It was just enough to make my spine tingle. I straightened my posture, took a deep breath and did something I had never really done: I stood up to Sally.

"I'm sorry you feel that way," I began, "It would be difficult if you were to be rude to our new employee during her first week with us."

Sally had been pushing her chair in, thinking that the conversation was over when she froze, her hands locked.

"What do you mean?" she asked, meeting my eyes for the first time.

"I mean," I said slowly and quietly, moving closer to the table. "I mean that I am hiring this girl. I am paying for her, and I am making the decision that she will stay."

I was shocked at myself when the words left my mouth. I could feel the momentum of the anger caused by my bruised ego building.

"You. . ." Sally stammered. "what money would you use?" I could hear the disbelief in her voice.

"Sally, I do make money in my job, you know. I do earn a salary. I do pay for some things around here, including your hair and nail appointments, your cigarettes, and that pretty little dress you're wearing," I said the last part eyeing her up and down and something about the way I was glaring at her made her blush. She lowered her chin slightly and smoothed the folds of her dress again. I took advantage of her moment of weakness and drove in a final nail.

"Besides, I've sat back for years and watched you and your parents make a mess of this situation. Obviously the three of you aren't qualified to choose our domestic help, and I am going to try my hand at it this time. I couldn't do any worse than you have already."

Sally had nothing to say in return. I think the shock of my resistance was already getting to her. She put a hand to her temple and began to massage it.

"Alright, dear," she murmured, the years of social etiquette taking control. She was going to do her best to be polite. "But I'm not well. I'm going to bed." I could tell she had one of her migraines coming on. In the past this would have made me capitulate to her wishes, but this time it merely irritated me.

"Fine," I said. "You do that. Tomorrow morning you can meet her and let her know what it is you'll be expecting from her."

Sally stood still frozen for a moment. I watched as her eyes glanced from my face to the screen door behind me and back to my face again. She was trying to get a read on why I was so adamant. What was it about this particular girl that would make me act this way? But I didn't even know myself. All I knew was that as I regained my strength, it began to get easier. I was happy she was going to bed, yes. I hoped that she would take a sleeping pill or two and go to sleep and not speak to me any more this evening. I stood unmoving, my fists clenched at my sides, waiting for another volley from her, but she seemed to have given up, at least for the moment.

"Goodnight then," she said, walking over to me and brushing her lips against my cheek.

I watched her go into our bedroom and shut the door, then I turned and opened the screen door for Melee to come inside.

"Well," I said to no one in particular, "that went fairly well."

Melee stepped just inside the door and began to peer around the kitchen. My wife had had it painted yellow. We had the latest appliances: a dishwasher, icebox, and electric stove, all in buttercup yellow. The Formica counter tops and the kitchen table were mint green. I rubbed my hands together and went over to the icebox, suddenly liberated with the fact that I could decide what to have for supper.

"Is there anything I can get you, Melee?" I asked, over my shoulder.

"Uh, yes sir," she said quietly. "A towel, please?"

I looked back at her. She was still soaked through, I had forgotten, and was beginning to drip a bit on the floor.

"Oh, yes, sure, of course," I sputtered. I went to the linen closet and pulled out some towels and washcloths.

"Here," I said, "let me show you where you'll be staying."

She grabbed her bag and followed me up the narrow staircase that led from the kitchen to the garconniere. At the top of the stairs, I reached up and pulled the string of a light bulb hanging from the ceiling. It was beginning to get dark outside, and the light swinging from the end of the string threw strange shadows on the walls. The north end of the garconniere was really used as our attic, and so she had to wade with me through the piled up trunks, the unused and broken furniture, the boxes of old photo albums and childhood keepsakes; things my wife and I had brought with us to our marriage and many things we had accumulated over the course of the past ten years. There was a central aisle that led through the general chaos to the door of a tiny room that had been walled in from the rest of the space. This was where our maids slept. As I opened the door, I felt for the first time that it was entirely inadequate. On one side of the room was an ancient bed with a tattered quilt and pillow. Next to it, a bedside table and reading lamp. Across from the bed, on the other side of the room was a rickety chest of drawers, and directly under the window a waist-high stand with a washbasin and pitcher.

"Well, this is it," I announced, attempting to make as much room as possible for her to walk inside. "It can get pretty hot up here in the summer time, so you'll want to leave the windows open up here, and you may want to leave your door open too so you can get the cross breeze."

She stood next to the bed, clutching her bag and taking in the room. She said nothing, and I filled the silence by walking over to her window and opening it up. The rain had died down to a gentle patter and I could feel the heat of the July day beginning to subside.

"I'll just go bring you some warm water so you can wash up a bit," I muttered, grabbing the pitcher from the stand.

I immediately felt stupid for saying it. The poor girl had been drowning in rainwater all day, probably the last thing she wanted was to get wet again, but she only nodded as I turned and left, crossing back through the attic. I opened the other window at the top of the stairs and then made my way back down to the kitchen. Instinct drove me to switch off the light. I had very little occasion to be up there, and it was automatic for me to turn off lights whenever I left an empty room.

At the kitchen sink, I stood trying to get the right temperature for the water and hoping it wasn't too hot or too cold for her liking. Again, I just couldn't shake the feeling that I wanted to please her; that I hoped that she would like it here and that she would stay. All of the other hired girls had not mattered to me at all. I didn't know the names of most of them. I only knew that they wouldn't be there long, that there would come a point when Sally would tire of them, either from an imagined failure in the kitchen or some other domestic duty or just from sheer boredom, and so I felt that it didn't really matter whether I knew their names or not. This time, however, I felt that somehow Melee needed to succeed. That somehow I needed her to do what no other house girl had been able to: keep Sally happy. Perhaps it was only because this time it had been my choice and I wanted to be right for a change. I wanted to be right.

I took the pitcher of warm water and began trudging back up the narrow staircase. By the time I got to the top I was winded, and so I stopped to catch my breath for a moment before I turned the light back on. The garconniere was dark now. The sun had gone down and the crickets and bullfrogs were beginning to warm up for their nightly concert. The only light came from the little lamp on Melee's bedside table. I could see the foot of her bed, and the window in her room, cut out in the frame of her doorway. At that moment, she walked into view, and turned to look out her bedroom window, rubbing a towel through her wet hair. She was naked.

Her skin was pearl white. It had a pale pink hue to it and seemed to glisten in the light. Perhaps it was just the rain she was toweling off, but the effect was bewitching. The muscles in her back rippled as she moved the towel through her hair and twisted her neck to get a good view of the sky. I was surprised that someone so small and delicate could have such powerful musculature. I imagined it was from the years of hard work in a cabin back in the woods where she would have carried water to wash and scrub the clothes in an old tub, chopped wood, cleaned fish, and lifted heavy cooking pots on and off the stove. Her strong shoulders and back dipped into a tiny waist and she had two dimples in the place where her back met her buttocks, round and firm.

I suddenly became aware that I had been there past the point of an honest mistake and now was becoming a voyeur. I sucked in a breath, hoping to reverse down the stairs and then walk back up, this time turning on the light and making enough noise so that she'd know I was coming, but she turned around before I could. I cringed, waiting for the scream, the slamming of the door, and the mortified tears, which should be the usual result of surprising a woman in the nude. Instead she moved the towel in front of her and stared at me with eyebrows arched in surprise. She did not seem the least bit embarrassed or confused. She just stood silent, expectant, waiting for me to speak.

"I, uh, brought you your water," I said, feeling ridiculous. Like a guilty child I held the pitcher up to show her.

She still did not move, and so I edged toward her, through the attic, holding out the pitcher in front of me, and trying not to meet her gaze. She backed up against the wall near the window, still holding the towel and still not showing the least sign of fear or humiliation. When I reached the little stand, I poured the water from the pitcher into the basin. I could feel my hands shaking, and concentrated on controlling my vision, staring straight down and watching the water slosh into the bowl.

"I expect you're hungry," I said. "You're welcome to come down to the kitchen and have something to eat. I believe we have some bread and some things for sandwiches."

I could feel my voice wavering in embarrassment. I felt idiotic, standing so close to her, feeling the warmth of her, and pretending that I didn't. I wondered why she was acting as if nothing were out of the ordinary. I felt the blood rushing to my cheeks, and quickly turned away so she wouldn't see me blushing. Then I walked out the door and closed it behind me.

When I reached the kitchen, I felt a madness coming over me. I knew that at that moment she must be dressing and getting her things together to leave. She had to be. I paced back and forth across the linoleum for a few minutes, wondering what I could say or do to excuse myself. I decided that the least I could do would be to drive her home. I was sure she must have come a long way. She might have started walking this morning. She had to live several miles south along the route of Bayou Teche, down past the town, past the Bottoms and out into the woods and swamplands. I wasn't even sure if my car could even take her as far as her house, some of the Cajun folk used pirogues to travel to their little shacks.

I crept to my bedroom door and cracked it open, hoping that my wife would be asleep. She was. The bottle of sleeping pills sat on her nightstand next to a glass of water. From the sound of her snores and the drool on her pillow, I knew that she had taken at least two. I would be safe to drive Melee as far as I needed to tonight and return without my wife ever knowing I'd gone. I gently pulled the door closed again, and returned to the kitchen. Not knowing what else to do, I poured myself a glass of milk and then sat at the table waiting for Melee to come down and then tell me that she wanted to leave.

I waited for what felt like a terribly long time. The crickets in the yard and the frogs out in the bayou had now worked themselves up to a full-blown roar. I watched a moth whirl and circle over my head, every now and then smacking into the kitchen light, flying back, whirling around and then smacking it again. He seemed to be trying to get inside it. I wondered what drove him to do it. What was it about the light that compelled him to keep trying, despite the hopelessness? Somehow to get inside and be encircled in the warmth and the light, to be a part of it, rather than just admire and appreciate it from afar, but the glass of the bulb repelled him, over and over.

The most he could hope for was the pain and the blindness that ensued. When I looked away, the light bulb was still burning in my eyes, and I closed them to try and take away the image. When I opened them, Melee was standing there in front of me.

She was wearing an old nightshirt. It seemed like it could have been her father's, it was so long and bulky. The sleeves were rolled up over her elbows and all the buttons were done up, except the top two. I had a view of the hollow in the front of her neck where a silver chain and pendant dangled. Her wet hair was combed and pulled back away from her face and her feet were bare. She did not at all act like she was expecting to leave. Instead she glanced from me to the ice box and back again, and I realized that she was hungry and was expecting to eat the sandwiches I had promised her.

I jumped up from my seat, and motioned for her to sit down, the disappointment washing away and being replaced by a feeling of joy and excitement. She was staying! At least for tonight and maybe tomorrow, and maybe for a while even. I wrenched open the ice box and stood staring at the contents for several minutes, trying to clear my brain enough to think of what I might need for a sandwich. I decided on ham and pulled an opened tin out, along with some mayonnaise and placed them on the table. I grabbed the bread from the breadbox and began slicing it. I pulled two small plates from the cupboard and put the bread on them and returned to the table. She took a plate from me and I waited as she smoothed some mayonnaise on each slice and placed a thick piece of ham between them. I then assembled my sandwich, and the two of us ate in silence.

I could tell she was very, very hungry. She was trying to take small bites, but she ate quickly, taking big gulps of air between each mouthful. I offered her a glass of milk and she accepted, swallowing that down too. Then I pulled out a pound cake and cut two thick slices off. I put one on her plate and one on mine and sat back in my chair to watch her finish eating. She was eating more slowly now, enjoying the taste of the pound cake – taking several bites and then a swig of milk. The pound cake crumbled on the tips of her fingers and the milk oozed from the corners of her lips. When she was done, she licked the crumbs off and wiped her face on the back of her hand.

"Tank you for the food, Mr. Palmer," she said.

"Please, call me Bram," I smiled, taking the plates and putting them in the sink.

"Here, I do dat," she said, standing up.

"No, no," I said. "It's alright, you're not officially employed yet. Tomorrow morning you can start with the duties around the house. Tonight you're simply my guest."

Melee's face twisted in confusion. It occurred to me that she might never have been anyone's guest before. Might never have spent a single day without working. She glanced from me to the sink and then to the stairs, as though she were thinking perhaps it best she go to bed if she wasn't required to do the dishes.

"Please," I said, motioning to the chair. She sat back down, clasping her hands tightly in front of her on the table and biting her lip, a quiet snort escaping her nostrils.

"I guess you were pretty hungry after your walk today," I said cheerfully, hoping to start a conversation.

"Yes."

"How far did you come?" I asked.

"Dono," she shrugged, "maybe five or six miles. I can't tell. It was raining so hard, you know." She shifted uncomfortably in her seat.

"Well," I said, hoping to put her at ease, "I do hope you'll be happy here."

"Tank you, Mr. Bram," she said.

"No, just Bram," I reminded her. She didn't answer.

"So how did you find out that we needed a new maid?" I asked.

"I din," she answered.

"Excuse me?" I was surprised by this.

"I din know you need a new girl. My papa saw de store and just decide to go der and axe. Der was no one else around when we got to town, de storm was so bad."

"Ah." I said. I was trying to deal with the impact that this had on my mind.

"Mr. Bram, do you mind if I go to bed now? I'm very tired," she said, with an exaggerated yawn.

"Oh, not at all," I answered, distracted.

She thanked me again for the sandwiches and then turned to go back upstairs for the night.

CHAPTER FOUR

My mother named me Amy Lee. I think it's a pretty name. It's sad that I never heard the sound of her voice calling me that. In giving me life, she lost her own. I was the only girl. The last child of six: five sons and one daughter. I was the daughter she never had, but that she had always wanted.

The midwife took me to her home after my mother died. I called her Marraine. Marraine was ancient, as old as the cypress trees that towered over her tiny shack. She called them her "ladies," and they did look like tall slender women with long wavy hair and wide skirts. She said the trees were her friends, and the little animals that lived in them -- birds, raccoons, possums, and squirrels – were her children. She was a small, stooped woman with charcoal skin and curly gray hair. Deep wrinkles encircled her dark eyes that could flash like lightening in her brief moments of anger, but were most often crinkled up in laughter. She had no teeth, but never seemed to care and smiled easily just the same. She wore a dingy housedress and slippers almost every day but Sunday when she would dress in bright purples and oranges and wrap her hair up in an elaborate tignon with long feathers. She was Creole, and she knew the mysteries of natural medicine. Her little hands, gnarled with arthritis, possessed extraordinary powers, but they touched me with tenderness.

Marraine was always traveling around, tending to sick people, helping women give birth and sometimes acting as a preacher for a wedding now and then. She took me everywhere with her, calling me her little helper and teaching me all that she could. Folks would pay her with dried beans, rice, cornmeal, chickens, eggs, whatever they had. Marraine would take this food and make meals every day for the family and friends who came to see her. We would take it out to the porch to eat with plates on our laps. After supper, someone would pull out an accordion and a rub-board and then they'd play Zydeco and we'd dance until very late until Marraine would have to say, "Get on home, now!"

On quieter nights, I would crawl up on her warm lap and snuggle into her arms as she sat in her rocking chair, sometimes snapping beans, sometimes sewing a little, and telling stories to those gathered there on her porch. I remember well the stories that Marraine told. They would help me to fall asleep, something I was afraid to do, because I had terrible nightmares. Every night, I dreamt that I was drowning.

Marraine told me that it was because of my sadness. She told me that the pain was drowning me. On night after I had woken up screaming, she came to my little cot and pulled me into her arms.

"Tite Melee," she smiled, "I'm going to tell you a story. It's a story about a family who lost a little girl, right about your age."

"What happened to her?" I asked, drying my tears.

"Well, petite, she died."

"Like momma died?" I whispered.

"Yes, like your momma died," Marraine pulled me closer to her, and I lay my head against her chest. "Shush now, and let me tell you the story." I got very quiet.

"After the little girl died, her family was very, very sad. They cried.

Almost all the time, they cried. Until one day, the mother had a vision."

"What's a vision?" I interrupted.

"Oh, a vision, that's like a dream you have, except when you're awake."

I thought about that for a moment.

"So, the mother, she had a vision. She saw many little children marching, all dressed in white and each one holding a candle. At the very end of that line of children, she saw her own little girl who was holding a candle too, but her candle was not lit. She was the only one who had a candle that wasn't lit. So, she went up to her little daughter, and she asked her, 'Sweetheart, why isn't your candle lit?'

And the little girl looked at her, and she said, 'Momma' she said, 'you're always crying for me. The Good Lord doesn't like for you to cry for me. You have to accept that the Good Lord took me. Every time you cry, your tears put out my candle.'"

"Is that what the stars are, Marraine?" I asked. "Are the stars the candles of all the people who have died and are up there with the Good Lord?"

"Ooo-yie!" Marraine chuckled. "Now, I never thought of that, Tite Melee, but you might be right. You might be right. Now, you gonna shush and let me finish this here story?"

I pressed my lips together and nodded, eager for her to continue.

"Well now, where was I? Oh yes! That little girl, you see, pointed to the other children, walking ahead of her and she said, 'the others, their parents have accepted their deaths.' And she said to her momma, 'Their parents don't cry, and so their candles stay lit. So, you mustn't cry for me like that. You must accept that God wanted to take me. He wanted me. I belong to God now.' And she said, 'He took me when he was ready, and so,' she said, 'you must accept this cross to bear.'"

When Marraine had finished the story, she petted my head for a while in silence, then she leaned in and whispered softly,

"Tite Melee, you must accept that God took your momma. You mustn't cry for her. If you do, you will put out your mother's candle and she won't have any light there in the after life."

I thought about my mother, alone in the dark. I decided to no longer cry for her. We sat in silence for a while longer. The fire in the chimney crackled and hissed. Finally Marraine reached into her pocket and pulled out something bright and shiny that sparkled in the firelight.

"Here," Marraine said, "This is a keepsake from your mother."

It was a silver necklace with a simple braided chain and an oval pendant. Engraved on the pendant was the face of a woman, her bent head covered with a scarf, her eyes closed.

"Your mother was wearing this when you were born. She prayed for you, up until the end of her life. I took this necklace after she died. It's yours now. You can wear it, and like that you will always have your mother with you."

She put the necklace around my neck, and I have worn it ever since.

***

When I was five years old, my father came and took me away from Marraine. I remember how I cried and clung to her, and she said "Shush, now," and wiped my tears with her apron and wiped her face with the back of her hands. She told me that she'd see me again real soon and that I mustn't cry. I needed to be a big brave girl and go see what it was like in the city and bring her back a present. She held me real tight for a moment and kissed my head and then she let my papa pull me away and put me in his truck.

My father drove me to Lafayette to live with my grandmother, my mother's mother. She lived in a big, fine house. I was scared and excited as we drove up to it. I had never seen a house so big. When we arrived, my grandmother came running out to the truck to meet me.

"Thank the Lord!" she cried, "Oh, darlin' I've been waiting so long to see you! Oh my, how pretty you are! How you do look like your momma!"

Grandmother held my hand and walked with me back to the house. She twirled me around and fussed over me.

"My goodness!" she laughed, "That dress is frightful! We need to get you some new clothes, child! We'll go shopping tomorrow."

She gave me a slice of lemon pie and a tall glass of sweet tea, and she chattered away to me as I sat across from her at the big kitchen table. I understood most of what she said, though my English wasn't very good then. Gladys, her maid, was busy washing some okra in the sink and she turned around and smiled at me from time to time.

"Gladys, doesn't she look just like her momma!" Grandmother cooed.

"Yes ma'am. I believe she do!" said Gladys. "She just so pretty!"

The next day, Grandmother took me to town and bought me several new dresses with matching hair ribbons and two pairs of shiny new shoes: one black pair and one white. I had my own room, with a pretty poster bed, a little white dresser, and a vanity with a mirror. It used to be my momma's room, and her old doll cradle and rocking horse were still there in the corner. Grandmother would brush my hair each night and wrap it in curlers and it was at these times that she would tell me about my mother.

"Your momma was so beautiful, and so smart!" she'd say. "She was the smartest one in her classes. She always wanted to be a schoolteacher, you know. She'd take her little dolls and her stuffed animals and she'd line them up and pretend to teach them their letters and numbers. It was just so cute! She would have been a good teacher."

I wanted to be smart like my momma, and so when Grandmother put me in school, I worked very hard. I went to the local Catholic school, and my little friends would meet me in front of my house and we'd walk there together, all dressed in our starched white blouses, plaid skirts and knee socks. Gladys made a lunch for me every day, and I'd carry my little lunch pail and books in my arms. At school I learned how to read and write English. We weren't allowed to speak French. There was one other little girl who spoke French like me, and sometimes she'd whisper to me across the aisle. I tried not to answer her, but it was just so good to be able to speak freely the language that I knew best. One day Sister Margaret caught us and gave us three sharp raps across our knuckles. After that, I never spoke it in school again.

My grandmother was proud of me. She called me Amy Lee, which was the name my mother gave me. She told me my father didn't know how to spell it, and so he wrote "Amelee" on my birth certificate, "but that's not your real name," she said, "your real name came from your momma, not your father. Don't you forget that!" I got the feeling that Grandmother did not like my father much.

Grandmother always took me with her to visit friends, and they all said that I was the prettiest little girl they had ever seen. I took dance classes, ballet and tap. Grandmother said that my momma was a wonderful dancer and showed me her toe shoes that she kept in the closet on the top shelf. I held them in my hands, the pink silk worn in several places, and thought of my mother whirling and twirling across the stage. I didn't understand why my beautiful, smart, talented mother decided to leave Lafayette and live way out in the country with my father.

"Grandmother," I asked one night while she was brushing my hair, "how did my momma meet my papa?"

Grandmother stopped brushing my hair for a moment. Her lips pursed as though she had eaten something sour. Then she sighed a great sigh.

"Well, I guess you would ask that eventually. Honey, your grandfather, my late husband, was an oilman. He worked mostly in Jennings at the oil field there, managing the men. He would go for several days at a time, sometimes the whole week, and come home on the weekends. Your momma and I used to visit him from time to time, you know, bring him fresh clothes if he needed them, maybe a basket of cookies and cake.

Your grandfather was so proud of your momma! He used to love to show her off and tell everyone that she was going to go to college and be a schoolteacher. She was the apple of his eye! She loved to visit him.

There were a lot of men who worked for your grandfather. Most of them were poor folk, Cajuns like your daddy who came to Jennings to get some work. Well, one day your momma was visiting your grandfather and your daddy started talking to her. He was older than her and he would flatter her and say sweet things to her, and she, being so young, thought that she was in love.

When your grandfather found out, my goodness he was mad! He told your momma she could never see that boy again, and she wasn't allowed to go and visit him at the field anymore. It was the harshest that your grandfather had ever been with her. Sometimes I think maybe he shouldn't have spoiled her so much when she was a young girl, because she just didn't take this punishment well at all.

We didn't know it, but your daddy started coming here to our house to visit her, and she'd sneak out at night with him, and then one day they just up and eloped! Went all the way to Arkansas where they could get married, because your momma was only sixteen. They were gone for three days. I was frantic, I tell you! Your grandfather had every lawman in the parish out searching for her. When she finally came back, she told me they'd gone up to Texarkana and got married by a justice of the peace there.

Your grandfather was furious! He turned her out of the house, though I begged him not to. Your daddy said it didn't matter, and that he'd find work and take care of them. For a while he was working here in Lafayette, but later that year, you know, the big crash happened, and there was no work for anyone anymore. So your daddy took your momma – my precious baby girl –

back to those swamps he came from!"

At this, grandmother started crying a little. I put my hand up on her cheek, and she kissed it, and then wiping her eyes, she continued,

"Well, I got letters from her from time to time. She tried to be cheerful in those letters, but I knew that it was hard for her. She wasn't used to working so hard. He had her doing the cooking the cleaning, you name it. They didn't have two pennies to rub together, and sometimes I'd send her a little money when I could. She kept having baby after baby too. I don't know how she managed it. And they were all boys. All boys! She wanted a little girl so badly. And when she knew she was going to have you she wrote to me. I still have that letter. Do you want to see it?"

A wave of excitement came over me. A letter from my momma! I could barely contain myself. Grandmother saw the delight on my face and grinned.

"Alright then, I'll just get it for you."

She went back to the closet in my room, reached up on the top shelf again and carefully pulled down an old hat box. She set it down on my bed and opened it gingerly. With trembling hands, she picked up an envelope from the top of a pile of letters, pictures, dried flowers, and other small treasures in the box. She pulled the letter from the envelope and handed it over to me. I took a deep breath and read it:

Dearest Mother,

I am writing to tell you some good news. I am going to have another baby, but this time, I am sure it will be a little girl! I want to name her Amy Lee. Don't you think that's a good name? I want to dress her all in pink and put pretty ribbons in her hair, just like I used to wear. Won't she just be a little doll? I hope that you and daddy are doing well. I wish that daddy would let me come and visit. Maybe he'll change his mind when he knows he's going to have a granddaughter! I so want to see everyone. I miss you and Daddy and Gladys so much. . .

The letter continued on, but Grandmother took it out of my hands. She smoothed the worn paper lovingly, and then put it back in the envelope.

"That was the last letter I ever got from your momma," she whispered. "I didn't know she had died until months after you were born. Can you imagine! I wanted to go and get you myself, but your grandfather was still too bitter and angry to hear of it. But, a little while after he died, I did come and find you, and so, here you are, child!" She gave me a hug and kissed my cheek.

"And now, young lady, it is very late and you have school tomorrow and need to go to sleep!" I nodded and sank down beneath the covers, so happy to know that my momma had wanted me! Grandmother tucked me into bed and then turned off the light.

I lived with my grandmother for five wonderful years. It was the summer after I turned ten, and I was eager to be starting the fifth grade in the fall. One day, Grandmother wasn't feeling well. She went and got in her bed, and Gladys told me she was alright and just needed to rest for a while. I read to her at night for a few days. But then, she seemed to get sicker and sicker, and in a few weeks, she was dead. It happened so quickly. I could not believe it. The funeral came and went and still I did not believe it. Gladys sent for my father. She didn't know what else to do with me, so she packed up my things and put me on the porch, and I waited there until my father drove up in his old pick-up truck to get me.

CHAPTER FIVE

The first morning after Melee came to stay with us, I woke up to the smell of fresh coffee and bacon frying in the kitchen. I am always amazed at how quickly the sense of smell can take me back to my childhood, and the memories invoked are never purely happy. Most of the time, I try to evict from my mind as soon as they enter, but this morning I allowed them to drift in and set up temporary residence. Lying in bed, I kept my eyes closed and saw a picture of myself as an eleven-year-old boy.

It was 1934, and my mother, my little sister Gracie, and I were living in Ida Mae Wilson's boarding house in Savannah. My father was on the road to Atlanta, trying to scrape together enough to buy more wares to sell, and he had left us behind. I didn't mind. It was one of the few times when I could rest from our nomadic existence. When I felt that we had a home, even if it wasn't ours.

My mother helped Mrs. Wilson with the cooking and the washing and in return she allowed the three of us to sleep on cots in a small bedroom next to the kitchen. I used to earn pennies searching through garbage cans and parking lots for empty coke bottles and sometimes run errands or deliver milk for shopkeepers. Mrs. Wilson made breakfast each morning for the boarders and anyone else who wanted to pay the 15 cents. The eggs came from the chicken coop in her back yard, and Mrs. Wilson would serve them up with grits, biscuits and strong coffee. Mrs. Wilson's sister lived on a farm near Americus, and visited on occasion, bringing bacon and ham from one of her slaughtered pigs. It was those times I loved the most, because my mother would hand me a biscuit with two small pieces of bacon tucked inside and send me to eat on the back steps. It was often the only meat I would eat for an entire week. I loved the way the bacon grease soaked into the biscuit, making the crumbs cling to my fingertips.

Sometimes homeless men, wanderers and vagabonds, would come to the back steps and eye up the food in my hands. They'd ask me if I had any left, and I'd send Gracie inside to tell our mother. Mrs. Wilson would come to the door, usually with a pie tin full of scraps and leftovers and hand it out to the men. They'd scrape every last bite, and then take a drink from the garden hose, before tipping their hats and going on their way.

Sometimes Gracie would perform for them while they ate. At six years old, she was a laughing angel child, her hair done up in curls so she could be just like Shirley Temple. She would beg me to take her to the picture show and sometimes I'd have enough to pay the 20 cents for both of us. She loved Bright Eyes, and she'd dance and sing "On the Good Ship Lollipop" to the delight of these weary, downtrodden men, many who had little girls of their own somewhere, waiting for their daddies to send home the money that never came.

One day Gracie was dancing around the kitchen and fell. She was crying really hard, and when my mother picked her up she noticed she had a fever, and carried her back to her little cot. She stayed there for days, complaining of a headache, and I would visit her and promise to take her to a picture show as soon as she got better. A few nights later, she tried to get out of bed for a drink of water, and fell down again. My mother called to me and told me to go and get the doctor. I saw the fear in her eyes and I ran. Running through the heavy Savannah night, the tears flooding my eyes, I didn't know what was wrong with little Gracie, only that the fear on my mother's face filled me with an emptiness worse than any hunger.

All the next day my mother was locked in the little room with Gracie and the doctor. Mrs. Wilson sent me outside with stern eyes and told me not to disturb them. It was killing me not to know. I was sick with worry and sat on the top of the back steps, glued to the screen door, waiting for any sign, any word, that little Gracie would be alright. Mrs. Wilson came to the back door with a can of dried corn and told me to go feed the chickens and clean out their coop.

It was a hot, smelly job, and I hated it. I was afraid of the chickens and how they would peck at me when I tried to gather the eggs up from under them. The rooster was even more terrifying, and I was careful to lock him out of the pen while I cleaned the coop. He would be furious and would strut up and down outside the wire, cocking his head to the side and spitting at me. It was the perfect job to give my mind a little peace from the worry that consumed me.

It's funny how quickly death can come. That day it came as I walked back toward the house carrying a basket of eggs, the filth of the chicken coop still on my hands. It came with the doctor walking down the back steps, pausing on the bottom one to wipe the sweat from his bald head with a handkerchief and donning his hat. He nodded at me and then back at the house, said he was sorry and then walked away. I didn't understand why he was sorry, but I felt the basket slipping out of my hands, saw the eggs falling, the eggs for tomorrow's breakfast falling to the ground and spilling out in a mess of white and gooey yellow. It came with the sound of my mother's wail from inside the house, and the sound of her stifling it, and when I ran through the back door and into the kitchen and burst through the door of our little room, no longer banned to the outside, I saw her sitting on the floor next to Gracie's cot, her shoulders shaking with her sobs. It came with the sight of Gracie's curly hair, plastered with sweat to her still little head, her lifeless hand extended out from the cot and held tightly in my mother's.

I wanted to pick my little sister up and carry her out of there. I wanted to take her to the picture show. I was sure that if she knew we were going to see Shirley Temple she would wake up and throw her arms around my neck and smile. But my mother turned around and saw me,

"Get out!" she screamed. "Get him out of here!"

And I felt the arms of Mrs. Wilson around my shoulders, pulling me backwards, pulling me back into the kitchen and trying to shush me, to let me know it was alright.

"It's the polio, honey, she couldn't breathe any more," she said, her voice cracking. "You can't be in there, honey," she soothed, "you don't want to get sick too." Mrs. Wilson shut the door, cutting off my view. It was the last time I ever saw my sister.

I felt myself easing back, the tears blinding me again, and then I ran out of the house and stayed away all night. When I returned the next morning, there was no trace of Gracie. Mrs. Wilson was scrubbing the back steps with bleach. There would be no breakfast, not until the house was sanitized. My mother was sitting on the back porch swing wearing her hat and gloves. Our suitcases were packed and arranged next to her feet, all except Gracie's. When she saw me, she stood up and grabbed our things, and I followed her out of the yard and down the road to the bus station. We got on the bus to Atlanta to find my father.

During the long, long hours of that bus ride, my mother and I did not speak. I kept glancing at her face, hoping to see some sign of emotion there, but she stared ahead of her, her face expressionless and vacant. Only now and then would she sniff and raise the edge of her handkerchief, gripped tightly in her gloved fist, to the edge of her eyes, sigh deeply, and continue gazing straight ahead. I wanted to scream and cry and bury my head in my mother's chest and have her arms around me. Instead I choked back my grief until it was a burning lump in my chest that made it painful to breathe.

Lying in my bed, I could still feel that burning sensation, and I rolled over, pressing my fist into my chest and taking a gasp of air. The sound of a frying pan clanging on the stove made me open my eyes. Sally wasn't there. I was relieved. I knew she was most likely dressing in the bathroom. She did not like anyone to see her the morning after sleeping pills until she had washed her face and put on make up. I sat up and threw on a bathrobe and then made my way to the kitchen.

Melee had her back to me, stirring grits in a pot on the stove. The table was set for two with my wife's white porcelain "everyday" plates and coffee cups. I sat down and turned my coffee cup over. Without a backward glance, Melee picked up the heavy coffee pot and carried it over to me. She paused for a moment, and I raised my cup. Her eyes did not meet mine as she poured the coffee, steaming hot and a deep rich brown.

I am always impressed by the many different colors of coffee, from maple to mahogany; the tones and hues as rich and varied as the faces of the colored people who lived down in the Bottoms. So many different colors, and yet little noticed by most of the men I encountered from day to day who read the world like a newspaper and always took their coffee black.

I put the cup to my lips and breathed in deeply, allowing the steam to open up my sinuses, clearing the sleep from my mind. Melee had returned to the stove and was now bringing a frying pan with scrambled eggs over to me. She spooned some onto my plate, and then placed a basket of hot biscuits and a bowl of grits on the table. When she had put the bacon tray down, she stood back and wiped the grease from her fingers onto her apron. I could see the color of her hair better in the morning light. It was the color of molasses, with a hint of red, and she wore it soft and wavy down to her shoulders.

"Did you sleep well?" I asked her.

"Yes, tank you. Very good." She said. "You like de food? It tastes good?"

"Yes," I said, and smiled, taking a big bite of eggs. "Very good."

She seemed pleased and relieved, and began to collect the pans and rinse them in the sink.

At that moment, Sally entered the room. I saw her taking in the scene: the breakfast table set, Melee rinsing the pans, me dipping a biscuit into my coffee, unshaven and still in my bathrobe. I saw her eyes narrow and her chin raise. She cleared her throat. Melee turned abruptly. She turned off the water and wheeled around, her back to the sink.

"Melee, is it?" asked Sally.

Melee nodded. "Yes, ma'am, dat's right."

"Melee, if you're going to be working here with us, there are a few things you need to understand. First, you do not serve Mr. Palmer and me in the kitchen. We do not eat any meals in the kitchen; that is where you eat. We will be taking our meals in the dining room."

I shifted uncomfortably in my chair, suddenly feeling conscientious. Melee glanced from Sally to me and then back again. I could see the confusion on her face for a moment, and then watched it replaced by an understanding. Sally was clearly the one in charge.

"Breakfast is at eight o'clock; dinner is at two, when Mr. Palmer comes home for his midday break; and supper is at seven."

"Yes, ma'am," Melee agreed.

"Second," Sally continued, "you will dress properly. You will pull your hair back away from your face, and you will wear a uniform. Our last girl left hers hanging on the back of the pantry door. You may wash it today, but I expect to see you wearing it tomorrow."

"Yes, ma'am," Melee bit her bottom lip and tugged at her hair. I could see her trying to pull it back, but it was not cooperating. "But, um, tomorrow ma'am," she began, "tomorrow is Sunday."

"Yes yes," Sally stammered, "so tomorrow you shall have the day off – I declare, starting work on a Saturday of all things – you may have Sunday off of course, but I shall expect you to wear a uniform on Monday," said Sally, flustered.

"Yes, ma'am."

"Each morning I will leave a list of chores for you to do," Sally continued, regaining her composure, "you can read, right?"

"Yes, ma'am," said Melee, her shoulders stiffening.

"For today, you may wash the linens and polish the silver set in the dining room. The supplies are under the sink. I will be riding with Mr. Palmer to town to do some shopping. We'll be back this afternoon."

With that, Sally marched out the back door to wait for me. I knew she was still angry, but to speak to her would be kicking the hornet's nest. With Sally it was better to let her simmer on her own. Eventually her carefully cultivated civility would kick in.

I finished my breakfast and then shaved and dressed for work. When I returned to the kitchen, it was clean. The dishes had been done and put away, and the Formica table and countertops were sparkling. I walked to the back door, still doing up my tie and saw Melee through the screen. She was filling the washtub from the garden hose by the garage, preparing to scrub clean the ridiculous maid's uniform and white apron my wife insisted she wear.

Sally was fussing over one of her rose bushes, the sweat beading up on the back of her neck and dampening her bleached blond hair. It was a typical July day in South Louisiana, already ninety degrees at nine o'clock in the morning.

"You're late for work, dear," said Sally over her shoulder, shearing a thorny branch off with a loud snap. "Daddy won't be pleased."

I hummed in reply and pecked her lightly on the cheek.

"Don't be late tonight. We're supposed to play bridge with Peg and Warren."

I hummed again, and then headed for the garage to get the car.

Peg Blanchard was Sally's cousin. Her husband Warren was the District Attorney for Canaan Parish. We played bridge with them every Saturday night, and always at their home. Sally was too ashamed to host them at ours.

For the first time in many years I did not dread my ride to the drugstore. I turned on the radio to a rock-n-roll station and was pleased to hear Jerry Lee Lewis banging on the piano. The sky was a brilliant blue, and the air felt a little cleaner after last night's rain. The water had collected in the potholes, and they were filled with little sparrows splashing in and out. I passed a snowy egret walking on the levee, his gullet full from a morning of fishing in the bayou. I slowed down as a sandpiper darted across the road. The Cajuns called them papabottes for the sounds they made, and claimed that eating them gave a person extraordinary amorous prowess -- a belief that had at one time nearly caused the bird's extinction, and perhaps explained the frantic way in which this one seemed to be running for cover from me, as if he knew what I was thinking.

I dropped Sally off in front of the grocery store and then drove over to Bordelon's. When I arrived, little Izzy Johnson was standing at the back door, hopping from foot to foot, a huge smile across his shiny brown face. Izzy was our delivery boy. At eleven years old, he reminded me of myself as a boy, happy to be busy, to be earning even a few pennies to take back to his mother down in the Bottoms. Izzy was proud of his second-hand bike with the large basket in the front. He would spend hours behind the store, polishing that bike and waiting for the next delivery.

"Mr. Bram, Mr. Bram!" he shouted as I walked up.

"Mr. Bram, did you get stuck in that storm last night? Ooo-eee that was a big one!" His eyes were wide with excitement.

"Yeah, Izzy, it was quite a storm."

"Yes sir, yes sir it was," said Izzy. "You got any deliveries for me today sir?" he asked.

"Well, now," I said, "let's go inside and see, alright?"

Izzy was visibly thrilled as I opened the door and motioned for him to come in. He waited near the lunch counter as I hung up my hat, put on my apron and walked to the front of the store to unlock the door and flip over the open sign. Mrs. Connolly was already there, waiting.

"Bout time you opened, don't you think?" she snapped, bustling past me faster than it was probably safe for any ninety year old to go.

"Indeed it is, eh Palmer?" said my father-in-law, appearing from his office with the cash drawer in hand. He glared at me, and then his face broke into an enormous smile as he greeted Mrs. Connolly. She pulled him into a discussion about the best solution for an upset stomach, which had evidently kept her up all night. I smiled to myself, thinking that it was more likely she was upset by the thunderstorm than anything, but I was grateful for the distraction she provided my father-in-law. It would delay the browbeating I was sure to get.

I went behind the register and pulled out the ledger we kept for delivery orders. There were three standing orders on Saturdays, in addition to anything that might be called in. I prepared the orders in brown paper bags and then gave them over to Izzy. It was not necessary to explain them to him. Although he couldn't read, he had memorized all our standing orders for the week and could tell whose was whose by the size and weight of the bag. He also had the delivery route committed to memory. The day's order would take him on a five-mile journey from the store north to the Savoy's rice farm, down to a couple of addresses in the Bottoms and then back to the store again. He would be back by lunchtime, and would then start on his afternoon route to deliver anything that had been called in that morning.

Once Izzy had gone, I went back to the storeroom to get started on some inventory work. It wasn't long before Bordelon found me and began his daily verbal assault.

"So, Palmer," he sneered, "how long was it before Sally sent that little Cajun bitch back home?"

I was always shocked at the crudity with which my father-in-law spoke with me. It was a complete change from the polite gentility with which he addressed all his customers, neighbors, family and friends.

"Charlie," I said, watching Bordelon stiffen. After ten years of marriage to his daughter, the man still hated it when I called him anything other than 'Mr. Bordelon.' "Sally was fine."

"Fine? What do you mean fine?" he barked, the smile suddenly fading from his lips.

"I mean that Sally was fine with it. She's going to give the girl a trial period."

Bordelon squinted his eyes and cocked his head at me. The predictable way in which he behaved had never been more amusing to me.

"Trial period, huh?" he scoffed. "We'll see about that. Won't take long, I'm sure." With that, he stormed off toward the front of the store to ring up Mrs. Connolly.

The rest of the morning passed pleasantly enough, mostly because Bordelon wasn't speaking to me. Around eleven I took my post behind the lunch counter and started pouring coffee and making grilled cheese sandwiches for the small crowd that gathered every day. As usual, Sheriff Boyle took his spot at the end of the counter. I poured him a cup of coffee and lit his cigarette, then turned to make him a ham sandwich.

"Afternoon, Sheriff," I heard a familiar voice say, "afternoon, Bram." It was Warren Blanchard. I turned and nodded a greeting.

"Coffee?" I asked.

"No thank you kindly," he said. "I'll take a coke."

I popped the top off and handed it over. He took a long swig and then set the bottle down.

"You folks have any trouble here last night?" he asked me.

"No, why?"

"Meyer's jewelry store was robbed," interjected the sheriff. "Junior and I spent the morning talking to Ira. He didn't go to Lafayette today. Seems that someone took advantage of that storm."

"How do you mean?" I asked.

The sheriff glanced sideways at Blanchard, who took another sip of coke and cleared his throat.

"No one was out of doors last night. Shops closed up early and people went home to wait out the storm. Someone broke into Meyer's jewelry store during the storm when no one was around to see it."

"What did they take?" I asked.

"Just a necklace with a pendant," said the sheriff. "It's odd, really, it was made out of platinum, so it was quite valuable, but that's all they took. Just one necklace that was sitting in the window display."

"What was on the pendant?" I asked, curious.

"Saint Anne," said Blanchard.

CHAPTER SIX

Meyer's was the only real jewelry store in Canaan parish, but it also attracted customers from the surrounding parishes because of the unique items that it carried. In particular, Ira Meyer catered specifically to his Catholic clientele. There was jewelry for every sacrament: from tiny gold St. Christopher baptism pins, to sterling silver and crystal rosaries, often placed in coffins in the hands of the departed. Canaan parish society also flocked to Meyer's for diamond engagement rings, gold and platinum wedding bands, and pearl necklaces for debutante balls.

Ira Meyer, his wife Ruth, and three daughters were the only Jewish family in Techeville. The store was never open on Saturdays. That was the day the Meyers would travel to the synagogue in Lafayette for Sabbath. While Ira Meyer was one of the wealthiest men in Techeville, the Meyers were not invited to participate in the town's social calendar. They were naturally absent from weddings and funerals, baptisms and first communions. They were excluded from membership in the local country club, were not asked to play bridge, and were not invited to parties. The Meyer girls did not attend the cotillions. They were married away to young Jewish men in Lafayette and New Orleans, and rarely visited their parents once they left home.

The isolation, however, did not seem to bother Ira, who greeted the world and the customers at his jewelry shop with a perpetual smile. I would often visit him on breaks from the drugstore – Meyer's was across the street – just to say hello and chat. The day before the storm I had done just that. Ira was setting up a window display, draping blue velvet over little columns of various heights and making attractive arrangements of his merchandise. That day, the centerpiece was the platinum necklace and pendant depicting Saint Anne.

"Tomorrow is her saint day," smiled Ira. "You know she is patron Saint of mothers? She waited a long time to have a child. She reminds me of Hannah, the mother of our prophet, Samuel. She also waited a long time to have a child, and then when she finally did have a son, she gave him up to God! Strong woman," he muttered to himself. "Strong woman."

I nodded in agreement.

"So you see," he continued, "there is always hope for you and your wife," he smiled. "Always hope if you have faith."

I decided not to argue with him. It wouldn't matter anyway; Ira was convinced that the world was a happy place and something good was always around the corner. I admired him for his unfailing optimism, and wished I could soak it up and somehow feel it myself, but the horrible things I had seen in my life made me bitter.

Sometimes I felt a stab of longing for my own mother. She did not give me up to God – she had given me up to war. There were no mothers where I had gone. No maternal compassion, no womanly tenderness -- nothing but men and their pride, their hate and anger. Nothing but the abuse and cruelty of Japanese soldiers, who felt that surrender at the hands of one's enemy was an absolute disgrace. In surrendering the Philippines, we Americans became little more than animals to them -- worse than animals. They marched us sixty miles across Bataan to Camp O'Donnell. Every day and sometimes during the night for almost a week, they marched us, with no food, no water, and no rest. They would beat you with the butt of a rifle if you stepped out of line. They would run a bayonet through you if you fell. They would slit your throat if you bent down to help a buddy. We were dying from thirst. There were beautiful, pure artesian springs just off the road, but we were denied them. We could see them, almost reach out and touch them, but we couldn't drink. We were desperate for that cool, clean water – our tongues swelled and split and the sun beat down on us every day, and still we couldn't drink. After a few days, some of the men went insane and began running toward the springs. They were shot in the back for their trouble.

One of the few times they did let us rest, I was sitting across from a soldier who appeared frantic. He told me he was a doctor, and he was carrying quinine and was trying to empty his pockets before a Japanese soldier searched and killed him. I stuffed a bottle in my pants. Later at Camp O'Donnell, when I lay down on the bare dirt floor of my barracks and the malaria seized me, made me feel like someone was wringing my guts and the fever made me delirious, those quinine pills saved me.

The abuse continued for years – prison in the Philippines, then the hell ship to Japan, when they crammed 1,500 of us into the hold, shoulder to shoulder. They crammed us so tightly that we couldn't sit. You could squat or stand, but you couldn't sit. There was no light, except for what trickled down from the tiny hatch, fifteen feet over our heads and the only way in or out. For twenty-three days they left us in the darkness and heat, fear and stink. Each day they would send down one bucket of water for 1,500 men. One bucket of water for 1,500 thirsty men. If you were lucky, you got about a teaspoonful. The latrine was an open tub, and if you had to use it, you had to crawl over the backs and heads of hundreds of men to get to it. I was unfortunate enough to be standing near it, and had to endure that festering reek for twenty-three days. When the Japs would occasionally lift the latrine out of the hold to empty it, the urine and feces would slosh down onto our heads. I was covered in filth, and would retch at the smell of myself.

The prison camp in Japan was worse. We were forced to build an airstrip: twelve hours a day of back-breaking labor, breaking stones with pick axes and carting them in wheel barrows. The rations were meager and mostly rice, but never enough to end the gnawing hunger that ate you from the inside. The rice diet caused blocked bowels in some of the men. My buddy Dave died from it. He crawled under our barracks like a wounded animal and wouldn't come out – just lay there moaning in pain until he finally died. I can still hear him.

They would beat you with rifle butts until you couldn't hear. They would slap and punch and kick you. If you tried to escape, they would kill every man in your squad. When we were finally liberated, we were weak with hunger and fear – like dogs who suffer from the cruelest of masters. They had made us into what they thought that we were. It was months before I felt like I could walk upright again, I had spent so long hunched over from pain and paralyzing fear. I felt tainted. I felt like I would never wash the filth from me. I thought that I would be like my friend Dave, and just crawl off somewhere to die.

When I met Sally, she was like a light – so pure and unspoiled. Her modesty and sweet nature made me know there was still good in the world. There was still morality and values and faith in God. Perhaps this was why I wanted her in the beginning. I thought through her I could regain my self-respect -- be a man again. How wrong I was. My life with Sally was just another kind of abuse. More time in captivity and deprivation, but a prison of guilt and loneliness -- an absence of happiness, and a constant gnawing hunger for love. Perhaps I was an idiot to think that Melee might be another chance for freedom, but somehow I needed to believe it. I needed to believe that she could liberate me.

I was thinking about her as I cleared up the plates and dishes from the lunch crowd. Warren tipped his hat at me and said he'd see me later at the bridge game. I was thinking about her as I wiped down the counter. I was thinking about her as I washed my hands and hung up my hat and apron.

"Mr. Bram, Mr. Bram!" Izzy's excited voice brought me back to myself.

"Yes, Izzy, how did the deliveries go?" I smiled.

"Oh, they went good, Mr. Bram. I got some tips!" he grinned, showing me a shiny quarter and two dimes.

"Mr. Bram," he said quietly, "is there any more deliveries for this afternoon?"

I shook my head. Most folks came in on Saturdays to pick up their things. It gave them a chance to get out of the house and there weren't many deliveries that day.

"Mr. Bram, do you mind if I do them dishes later?" he asked.

"Hmmm," I teased, "it wouldn't be because there's a Western on at the matinee and you want to go?"

Izzy broke out into a broad smile. "Yes, sir!" he grinned.

"Well, I suppose those dishes can wait," I laughed. "Just be sure to be back here by three o'clock, right? I don't want Mr. Bordelon to fuss at you."

Izzy's face turned serious for a moment. "Yes sir!" he shouted. Then he gave a little yell of joy and ran out the door to the matinee.

I watched him go, pleased for a moment to see someone else so innocently happy. It reminded me of little Gracie and the way she would skip next to me, all the way down to the picture show.

"Daddy!" I heard Sally call from the front of the store.

"Sugar!" said Bordelon, giving my wife a hug and a kiss on the cheek. "How's my girl?" he smiled in paternal pride.

Sally launched into an accounting of her day's shopping and all she saw and did. The conversation was nearly identical to every Saturday. I took the opportunity to sneak out the back door for the car. I then drove around to the front of the store, honked the horn twice, and got out to open the door for Sally. She was still lingering inside, chatting away to Bordelon who continued to smile and nod with interest. I opened the door to the store and cleared my throat.

"Time to go, dear," I said, making a show of looking at my watch. I grabbed her shopping bags and took them out to the car. Sally followed me shortly afterwards, a loud sigh and a roll of her eyes let me know I had interrupted her.

We drove home together in silence.

Sally hopped out of the car as soon as we arrived. I took my time unloading the packages. The July sun was beating down into the yard. The clothes line was hung with freshly washed sheets – pure white – and the sun's reflection off them was blinding. I stood for a moment watching them flap like sails in the breeze. Melee's dingy gray uniform was also hung there, a lonely skiff floating in a sea of white. As I walked up the path to the back of the house, Gabriel Johnson's smiling brown face appeared.

"Hello, Mr. Bram," he smiled.

"Ah, Gabriel," I answered, "how are you? How's your mother?"

We exchanged pleasantries for a few minutes. Gabriel was Izzy's older brother. At sixteen, Gabriel was a tall, lean, strong young man. He'd been working for us since he was Izzy's age: mowing the yard, trimming the bushes, performing odd jobs around the house – things that I couldn't do, since my time was taken up at the drugstore. He was a good kid – smart and funny – and he wanted to go to trade school one day and become a carpenter. Like Izzy, he was pleased to be able to help out his mother at home.

Gabriel's father was a sadistic alcoholic. He no longer lived at home and spent most of his time wandering from place to place, trying to earn just enough here and there to keep himself drunk. When he did live at home, he would beat Gabriel and his mother almost every day, until one day he beat his wife unconscious and almost succeeded in strangling Gabriel. Izzy came running into the drugstore. It was lunchtime and he was crying. Six years old, he came in crying and begging for help. I saw myself in his face – the panic and fear – it was the same panic I had felt the day my mother sent me for a doctor for Gracie. I can't imagine the courage it took for Izzy to do it, but he ran up to Sheriff Boyle who was eating his lunch at the counter, and pulled on his sleeve:

"Please Mr. Sheriff," he said, trying to fight back his tears, "please sir, please come to my house, my daddy's going to kill my momma and my brother Gabriel."

Boyle had stiffened and took another sip of his coffee, "well now," he said, barely acknowledging the boy, "I guess some folks just ain't got no manners. I'm trying to eat my lunch right now."

Izzy was desperate. He was trying so hard not to cry, trying to be a man when he was only a little boy. "Please sir," he tried again, "I'm sorry to ask you, sir, but my daddy's going to kill my mama. He done knocked her to the floor, and he's choking my brother."

Boyle turned and studied him out of the corner of his eye. "Well, alright," he said, "I guess I can go down there and take a look, soon as I finish my lunch."

I was watching him and little Izzy, whose face fell. I saw the hope destroyed. It made my stomach lurch and churn. At that moment, I took the sheriff's plate and coffee cup, turned and stacked them in the sink.

"Lunch counter's closed." I said, folding my arms.

Boyle glared at me. Grabbing his hat, he crammed it on his head and then stormed out the door with Izzy following close behind. Perhaps it was his rage at me that made Boyle decide to throw Vernon Johnson out of town that day. After he'd done it, he proudly recounted how he'd marched into that shotgun house, stepped over Annie Johnson's beaten body and slammed Vernon on the back of the head with the butt of his gun. The blow knocked Vernon to the floor, and in doing so, made him release Gabriel's throat. The boy was purple and gasping for breath. Boyle grabbed Vernon by the hair and dragged him back outside. By that time, a crowd of neighbors had gathered in the front yard, stunned and speechless no doubt, to see a white sheriff intervening in what was usually considered a colored matter. Boyle threw Vernon into the back of his cruiser and then drove him out past the town limits and dumped him there.

"I kicked that son of a bitch in the stomach a few times," said Boyle proudly, "and then I told him I better never see his mangy nigger ass in my town again!"

It had been five years, and Vernon Johnson had not been seen in Techeville.

After the incident, I did what I could to help Annie Johnson and her boys. I started Gabriel cutting my grass and doing odd jobs and soon he was doing the same for our neighbors and friends. When Izzy was old enough, I gave him the delivery job at the store. I paid them both from my own meager salary. Sally told me I was ridiculous to do so, saying that nothing would change and eventually Gabriel would end up just like his daddy. I didn't care.

Gabriel had just finished mowing the lawn and was starting to sweep the sidewalks. He was hot and the sweat ran down his face and neck. At that moment, the back door opened and Melee appeared, holding a tall glass of lemonade. When she saw me, she seemed confused and almost a little afraid. She stood for a moment at the top of the steps, and then made her way down.

"Ah, Gabriel, this is Melee, our new house girl," I stammered, noticing that I was staring at her longer than necessary.

"Oh, yes sir," smiled Gabriel, "I, uh, met Miss Melee earlier today. When

I got here," he fumbled a little with the handkerchief he had pulled from his pocket and wiped the sweat off his forehead.

Melee cautiously handed Gabriel the lemonade, "It's so hot," she murmured, "I thought you might like something."

Gabriel grinned and nodded, "Thank you kindly. I do appreciate it."

She watched him as he drained the drink all at once, and then took back the empty glass.

"Lunch is almost ready," she smiled at me briefly, and then turned and walked back to the house.

I waved at Gabriel, who was picking up a broom and beginning to sweep the sidewalk, and followed Melee into the house. The screen door creaked loudly.

"Hey Gabe," I shouted over my shoulder, "give this door a grease, would you?" Gabriel smiled and returned my wave, and then went back to his sweeping.

Walking in the door, I was hit by an aroma I hadn't smelled since I was a boy: red beans simmering on the stove. My mother used to make them all the time, mostly because they were so cheap and easy to come by. Nevertheless, she took pride in making them: soaking them overnight, sautéing a little celery, onion and green bell pepper and then adding the beans and simmering them for hours, until they were creamy and tender. The smell would fill the house and cling to my clothes, maddening me to the point where I would have to go outside and wait patiently for dinnertime, when she would call me in after my father returned home.

"Gloria, I would rather eat your beans and rice than a steak dinner any day!" my father would croon. I had to agree. Those precious few evenings I would go to bed with a full stomach and a happy heart.

I stood in the kitchen, remembering my mother standing at the stove, stirring the beans. I watched Melee as she opened the oven door and removed a steaming pan of corn bread. When she turned around, her face was red and wet with perspiration. She set the pan down on the counter and began to cut carefully around the edges, releasing the corn bread from the pan and then dumping thick square slices into a breadbasket lined with a red and white checked napkin. She noticed I was staring at her, and self-consciously tucked a stray hair behind her ear.

"I can serve this up if you're ready," she smiled, waiting for a movement from me, which did not come. "You can go sit down now."

I pulled myself away from staring at her and went through the swinging door to the dining room. Sally was already seated. She was sipping at a glass of water and staring directly in front of her. I sat down across from her, noticing that she did not seem to blink. Her gaze went through me, focused somewhere on the wall behind.

"Smells, good, huh?" I attempted at small talk.

Sally did not respond. Melee came in with a large bowl of rice. The steam from the rice slowly began to fog up the large gilt-framed mirror directly behind Sally's head. In it, I watched Melee bending toward me as she spooned the rice into my bowl, her breasts swaying slightly underneath her blue dress, the same faded dress she had worn the day before, it must have dried over night. I realized that she was wearing neither a girdle nor a brassiere -- those stiff undergarments that most women of my wife's generation wore like armor. As she leaned over me, her breathing quickened. I looked up and saw the little hollow at the base of her neck. In the shadow there glistened a hint of the silver necklace I'd seen her wearing last night.

"My, my," Sally interrupted my thoughts, "I guess it must never get hot down in those cool backwoods swamps, now does it?" Her tone was harsh and penetrating.

"Pardon me, ma'am?" asked Melee, her hands beginning to shake.

"Well now," said Sally, smiling like a shark, "I just meant it certainly is strange to be making hot beans and rice in the middle of this July heat! But I suppose, that doesn't bother you, uh, Cajun people, right?"

Melee was confused and terrified. She didn't speak for a moment. I glanced across the table and saw the victory in Sally's eyes.

"Oh, no, sorry ma'am," Melee stuttered, "I uh, I mean, der wasn't anything to cook, you know? All I could find was some cornmeal, some rice and some dried beans in the pantry."

"That's quite alright." I smiled, reassuringly. "I'm sure it's just fine."

Defeated, Melee trudged back to the kitchen and returned momentarily with the beans and cornbread. As she was spooning the beans for Sally, I watched her shake nervously, the serving spoon clanging against Sally's bowl. Her silver necklace fell out from the top of her dress. I watched her quickly stuff it back.

"Pretty little necklace," remarked Sally, the edge of sarcasm cutting her voice. "Don't see too many of those in the swamp, now do you?"

"Yes, tank you," whispered Melee, "it was my mother's. She gave it to me, when she died."

Sally dropped her eyes. I could see the color come to her cheeks and knew that she was embarrassed for being uncivil. Melee finished serving and then left us alone in the dining room.

CHAPTER SEVEN

I didn't try to speak to Sally for the rest of the meal. I had a hard time swallowing down my food, even though it tasted delicious. Sally disgusted me. As soon as I took my last bite, I stood up and pushed my chair away from the table.

"Bram," she started, gazing up at me, I could see a softness in her eyes that I hadn't seen in a while. At one time it would have melted me. Today, it only made me feel more disgusted.

"Damn it, Sally," I sneered, "you can live out your days being a shriveled up, bitter old woman, but don't you dare hate that girl just cause she's got a little life left in her."

For a moment, I was stunned at myself, hardly recognizing my own voice. It was the harshest I had ever spoken to Sally. I did not dare see its impact on her face, fearing that her expression would soften my resolve. Instead, I stormed out of the house. Melee was nowhere around. Gabriel was still there, getting a drink of water from the garden hose.

"I greased up that hinge for you, Mr. Bram," he said.

"Yeah, yeah, thank you Gabe," I answered, distracted.

"Miss Melee's real nice," he said. I shot a quick glance at him, surprised that he seemed to guess my thoughts.

"Yeah, uh, I guess so," I hedged, trying to sound nonchalant. "Well, I'd best get back to the store."

"Yes sir," he smiled, "I'll see you Monday."

I took one last look around for Melee, and then jumped in my car to head back to town.

I spent the rest of my day thinking about her.

When I returned to the house to collect Sally, she had regained her steely composure. Whatever her feelings about what I had said to her that day, she didn't show it.

We drove in silence to the Blanchards'. Warren R. Blanchard, Jr. was a third generation district attorney. His father, Warren Senior, and his grandfather, Royce Blanchard had both been district attorneys for Canaan parish. There had been a Blanchard in the office for so long that voters simply checked the name on the ballot automatically. Junior, as Warren was called by most of his family and friends, fully expected his son, Warren R. Blanchard, III, or Trey as he was called, to take up the family business one day as well. I sometimes chuckled to myself at the Blanchards' attempts to emulate royalty. If Trey had a son, he would undoubtedly be named Warren R. Blanchard, IV. I secretly wondered what his nickname would be.

Sally was the only one who called Junior by his first name. They were friends growing up and high school sweethearts, and everyone thought that they would marry, but Sally insisted on going to college. Blanchard, like Sally, was not used to waiting for anything he wanted. After Sally left, he settled on Peg Landry, Sally's closest cousin. Peg and Sally were the same age, and had been debutantes together, but where Sally was a stately and graceful magnolia, Peg was more like a Louisiana iris, growing wild and free along fences, around mailboxes and in road-side ditches from Alexandria to New Orleans. Junior and Peg drank and partied together at honky tonks, and Junior took out his longing and frustration on Peg in the backseat of his car. Their hasty marriage raised more than a few eyebrows in Canaan parish, and Trey was born six months later.   Once they were married, Peg settled down to the task of all good Catholic wives: having lots of children. Trey was now eleven, and three-year-old Mary-Alice was the youngest of five. Peg was heavily pregnant with their sixth.

When we arrived at the Blanchard home, Peg waddled out the front door to greet us. She worshipped Sally and didn't seem to mind that her husband still ogled her cousin with a schoolboy's crush. To Peg, Junior was rightfully Sally's and it was only by the grace of God that she had somehow managed to end up Mrs. Warren R. Blanchard, Jr. Instead of jealousy, Peg seemed guilty to have the life she led, and constantly tried to compensate. She had made Sally her maid of honor, godmother to two of her children, and her closest confidant and friend. She rarely made a decision without asking Sally's opinion first, and she was never happier than when Sally was sitting beside her.

"Sally, darlin'!" Peg cooed, holding out her arms wide and catching my wife in a long hug. "I declare, you look more beautiful every time I see you, don't she look beautiful, Junior?" Peg called over her shoulder to Blanchard, who was standing in his doorway.

I could see that it wasn't difficult for him to agree. I, on the other hand, had become immune to my wife's beauty and charm. For me, they were simply the mask she wore to hide the years of resentment and bitterness at the unfortunate life she had chosen.

"Come on, Sally," Peg beamed, "I want you to see these swatches I got, I'm trying to pick out some new curtains for the master bedroom." Sally and Peg walked arm and arm into the house and I followed behind.

"Evenin' Bram," grunted Blanchard.

"Evenin' Junior," I nodded back.

He led me into the sitting room, where a card table was set up and a buffet laden with much more food than necessary for the four of us. It was the usual fare: cold cut sandwiches, party mix, and potato salad.

"Martini, Bram?" asked Blanchard. I nodded in assent and took a seat in one of the two white damask armchairs. Blanchard took a moment to shake a couple of martinis and then brought me a glass. I slowly sucked the olive off the toothpick and then used it to stir the liquid around a bit. Blanchard and I sat in silence. Both of us accepted the charade that our wives forced us to play every Saturday night. After ten years, we had nothing left to say, but quietly tolerated each other's presence for the sake of Peg and Sally.

"Junior!" gasped Peg in mock horror, "my, my, where are our manners, you haven't offered our guest any food yet?" she was flushed with pleasure, having secured Sally's advice on the important choice of curtain for her bedroom.

"I just knew you'd choose the country floral, didn't I tell you she'd choose the country floral?" Peg chattered away. She didn't wait for her husband to respond. "Well, that settles it, and I want them in Priscillas, right Sal?" she fretted. Sally nodded. It amused me to think that Peg could not even say what she wanted without Sally's confirmation.

Peg shooed all of us over to the buffet table. We grabbed plates and began serving ourselves. Blanchard made two more martinis for Peg and Sally and the four of us sat down around the coffee table, plates on our knees. Sally and Peg sat side by side on the divan, and Blanchard and I faced each other in the two white armchairs. We were about to settle in to our meal, when there was a quiet knock at the sitting room doors.

The door was opened by a small-framed colored woman wearing a maid's uniform. It was Annie Johnson.

"Annie!" gushed Peg, "are the children ready for bed, then?" she asked.

"Yes ma'am," answered Annie, "all bathed and ready for Sunday mass," she smiled. "The children would like to say goodnight to y'all if that's alright."

"Of course! Come in, darlins," Peg called.

The five Blanchard children trooped in like little soldiers, oldest to youngest, all with slightly damp hair, wearing their pajamas, robes and slippers: Trey, Sarah Beth, Landry and Jimmy. Mary-Alice, the youngest, was carrying her teddy bear. Each child walked around to each of us, giving us a kiss on the cheek and saying good night. It was equal parts charming and nauseating. When it was Mary-Alice's turn, Blanchard scooped her up onto his lap and tickled her. She started giggling uncontrollably.

"Junior, stop it!" Peg scolded, "You'll get her all riled up and she won't be able to sleep!"

"No he won't, momma!" cried little Mary-Alice, still giggling, clearly delighted by the special attention.

"Ok then, girl," sighed Blanchard, "You listen to your momma. Off to bed you go!" He set her down and then gave her a gentle pat on the bottom. She jutted out her lower lip and followed her siblings out the door.

"I declare, that little girl is the apple of her daddy's eye!" giggled Peg. "I don't know what she'll do if this one is another girl," she patted her huge pregnant belly. "She may not be the little princess any more. Oh, and Sal, if it is another girl, I think we'll name her Charlotte, for Grandma Landry, what do you think?"

Before Sally could answer, there was a quiet cough from Annie.

"Excuse me, Miss Peg," she murmured, "I think I'll go after I put the children to bed, if that's alright with you."

"Of course!" answered Peg. "We'll see you Monday morning. Oh, and happy birthday, dear."

We all joined in wishing Annie a happy birthday. She smiled and nodded and then quietly closed the doors. I thought about her long walk back to the Bottoms. She would not be home before nine o'clock, and she would be back by six in the morning on Monday. Annie Johnson had come to work for the Blanchards not long after her sadistic husband had been run out of town. She acted as cook, maid and nanny to them Monday through Saturday, only taking Sunday off to be at home. Izzy had only been six when his mother started working, and the Blanchard children had spent more time with her than he had in the past five years.

"I declare, I don't know what we'd do without Annie," sighed Peg. "Sal, did you find a new maid?"

Sally glanced from Peg to me and then back to Peg. I saw Blanchard stiffen.

"Well, Bram brought someone home with him yesterday," she mumbled, studying her cards. "A Cajun girl."

Peg raised her eyes in surprise. "A Cajun girl? My, my, that's different. Are you sure about that, Bram? I mean, can you trust her?"

"She's given me no reason not to," I grumbled, feeling a little irritated.

"Did you get any references?" Peg asked, "I mean who is she?" She was clearly shocked.

"Her name is Melee Mouton," I replied, "and she made some mighty fine beans and rice for us today."

"No, she's got no references," Sally spoke up. "Bram wants to see how things go for a while."

Blanchard chuckled. "That's a new one, eh Palmer?" he sneered. "I try my best not to mess with the affairs of women, and choosing the help is certainly one of them. I guess they don't give you enough to do at the drug store." He laughed and took another sip of his drink.

"Beans and rice!" cried Peg marveling at the novelty, "Sal, be careful of that Cajun food, those spices aren't good for one's constitution, if you know what I mean," she giggled nervously, but stopped when she saw the redness growing in Sally's cheeks.

"Well, I suppose it's none of our business," she frowned.

After we'd finished our meal, the four of us took our places at the card table. Sally and Blanchard always played as partners, as did Peg and I. Peg's bridge play was terrible, and we inevitably lost. She frequently drank too much and was far too distracted trying to chat with Sally to really pay attention. This evening Peg was on her fourth martini by the third auction.

"Junior," she slurred, taking a drag of her cigarette, "tell Sal and Bram about Meyer's!" she tapped Sally on the elbow to get her attention, pleased she had remembered a titillating topic of conversation.

"Margaret Landry Blanchard," sighed her husband, shaking his head, "You know I can't discuss my cases."

"Oh come on, honey!" she whined, poking out her lower lip. "Sally wants to know, don't you, Sal!"

Sally shifted in her chair, "Warren, you don't have to tell us if it's confidential."

"Well, I suppose I could," he smiled. "Long as we keep it in the family, right Palmer?" he slapped me on the back much harder than necessary.

Blanchard launched into the story of the robbery at Meyer's jewelry store to the delight of Peg and obvious interest of Sally.

"Who do you think did it, Warren?" asked Sally, her eyes wide.

"Don't have a clue," he answered, adjusting the cards in his hand. "Whoever it was, they had to be a small person."

"How so?" I found myself asking. The mysterious tone in Blanchard's voice had caught my attention.

"They broke into a side window, no more than a foot tall and two feet wide. But you know, the strangest part was this window is about seven feet off the ground. It was too high for someone to climb into themselves. They must've had a boost to get in."

We all sat in silence for a moment, thinking about this scenario.

"What did they take, Warren?" whispered Sally.

"A platinum necklace!" Peg chimed in, pleased to be able to add to the conversation.

Blanchard sighed again. "Yeah, it was a platinum necklace that was in the window display. It had a Saint Anne pendant on it. It was quite valuable, according to Ira. It'll be a felony if we ever try the thief."

I watched Sally as she sat pondering this. I thought I saw a flicker of recognition move across her face.

By ten o'clock we were all heavy lidded, and Peg was beginning to nod off.

"I think it's time we left," Sally turned toward me. I agreed, only too ready to end the evening, and moved to stand up.

"Oh, no, no," pleaded Peg, willing herself awake.

"You need to get some rest, in your condition," soothed Sally. She gave Peg a kiss on the cheek.

The Blanchards walked us out. Peg covered Sally in sloppy hugs and kisses. Junior shook my hand, squeezing for just a moment longer than I liked, his heavy gold class ring crushing my knuckles.

"You're keeping Sally happy, right Palmer?" he muttered under his breath, the smile frozen on his face.

"Yeah, sure," I stammered, a little taken aback, "I try my best."

"Well maybe you'd better try a little harder." The malice in his voice was unmistakable. I looked into his face and pulled my hand out of his. He winked at me and slapped me on the back. Again I felt the painful thump of his ring.

I thought about what he had said as I drove us home. Blanchard had made it clear to me on many occasions that he did not find me worthy of Sally. I was an outsider, a gentile in the Old Testament sense of the word. Blanchard did not like to lose. He had an undefeated record as a prosecutor, helped largely by the understanding he shared with Sheriff Boyle. If Blanchard wanted a conviction, Boyle made sure the evidence was there to provide it. It was only my covenant with Sally that protected me, and Blanchard reminded me of that every chance he got.

Sally stared out her open window into the night. The bullfrogs' loud croaking accompanied us along the way. The sound was hypnotic and numbing. It filled the night with an unseen menace. As soon as we got home, Sally went straight to bed without a word. I knew that she'd be taking a sleeping pill or two. I was too keyed up to go to sleep, and so I went out to the screened-in back porch, sat down in one of the wicker chairs, pulled out a cigarette and lit it up.

I had just finished smoking and was leaning back in my chair when the kitchen screen door opened. It was Melee. She walked out onto the back porch and stood staring up at the moon. She did not see me, and I guessed that she must have assumed I had gone to bed. Her dark hair was hanging long and loose around her face. She was wearing that old bulky nightshirt again. The moon reflected strangely off her bare arms and legs, as though the light came from inside her. I struggled to regulate my breath that was now coming harder and faster from my chest.

Melee stretched and yawned, her arms reaching up over her head, lifting the bottom of her nightgown high enough that I could see a hint of her milky thigh. She finally sat down in the old creaky rocking chair near the kitchen door and began to hum softly to herself, the groan of the rocking chair keeping time with her song. Soon she was murmuring words I didn't recognize. I strained to hear, and realized that she was singing in French. For a moment I was surprised, and then remembered again that this was language she had been taught from infancy. It was not often one heard Cajun French spoken. The Cajuns kept mostly to themselves, retreating from the hostility that the English-speaking world had assailed them with since their ancestors had been chased out of Canada. I didn't know much of their painful history, except that it had driven them far back into the swampy woods and forgotten backwash of the Mississippi river, too wild and uncivilized for the genteel tastes of the cultured, but a refuge for these pilgrims who wanted nothing more than to live in quiet tranquility. The years of persecution had made them shy in the English-speaking world, reluctant to betray their heavy accents that left them so often open to ridicule. Those who attempted to assimilate were even worse off. Cajun children who attended schools were forbidden to speak French, even to each other, and were punished severely if caught doing so.

Melee continued to sing softly, the tone of her voice mixing perfectly with the bullfrogs' croaking, the drone of the crickets, and the steady groan of the old rocking chair. It lulled me into a deep sleep, and I spent the night dreaming of old broken-down cabins, gentle faces peering out from porch swings, singing soft melodies in words I did not understand, and the moon shining like Melee's glowing skin on bayou water, as deep and green as her eyes.

CHAPTER EIGHT

All the stories they tell children are not happy. Some are about monsters and ghosts and creatures that live deep in the swamps. I remember another story Marraine told me: the story of the Vieux Diable.

One day I was crying, and I asked, "Marraine, why doesn't my family want me?"

"Because they are jealous of you," she muttered. She was busy sewing a shirt and rocking herself on the front porch.

I was shocked. This was news I had not anticipated.

"Jealous? Why are they jealous?"

"Because you're the youngest," she said, pulling a knot through her thread to end a stitch. She looked over at me and could see from my face that I did not understand.

"Tite Melee," she sighed, "have you ever heard the story of Petit Poucet?"

"No Marraine," I shook my head. "Who's Petit Poucet?"

"Well, now, that's a story! Come here and listen good, my dear."

She put her sewing aside and I climbed up into her lap, prepared to listen.

"Now, there was a family, and like your family they had many children, and the youngest one, they called Petit Poucet. Petit Poucet was smarter than the others, and he was loved the most by his daddy and momma. Since he was the youngest, they had more time to play with him and love on him than the others, and his brothers and sisters were jealous of him."

"But Marraine," I interrupted, "my momma and papa, they don't love on me. I never even seen them."

"Melee," Marraine scolded, "you gonna listen to my story or not?"

I sighed and nodded my head. I was not convinced that this story should apply to me, but Marraine was usually right.

"Alright then," said Marraine. "Now, one fine day, the children got together and the oldest one said, 'We should do something about him. What shall we do?' They could not stand their little brother! It seemed he always got the best presents and they thought he was loved more than they were loved. They didn't like it and decided to do something about it. So, they took the wagon and hooked up the horses and went into the woods. And Petit Poucet, he, he was smart now, like I told you. He guessed what the others were doing. And when he saw them together, he hid himself and spied on them and listened to what they said so he knew when they wanted to go in the wagon that they were going to do something with him. He filled his pockets with some rocks and he sat in the back of the wagon, and every now and then he would drop a rock on the ground. All along the way he dropped rocks."

"Why did he do that?" I interrupted again.

"You'll see, child, you'll see," Marraine chuckled. "So now, those children took that wagon way back into the woods, and then stopped at a place where Petit Poucet had never been. His brothers and sisters pretended to take a walk then, and when they were a little distance away, they all ran and got back in the wagon. They ran so that Petit Poucet couldn't catch up with them, and they left their little brother all alone in the woods. He searched and searched for the way back. He searched for those rocks, but couldn't find them. He was lost!"

I shuddered. Being lost in the woods was something I dreaded. There were too many creatures living out there, and no matter how many times Marraine said I had nothing to worry about, the hair still stood up on the back of my neck whenever I had to go to the outhouse in the middle of the night.

"So then," continued Marraine, "Petit Poucet saw a house and he said to himself, 'It's almost night time. I'm going to take a chance and go to that house. If I sleep out here in the woods, the bugs will eat me up, and I'll be scared all by myself.'

He went to the house and called. The mistress came out. He told her what the trouble was, how his brothers and sisters had brought him way out into the woods and how he was lost and couldn't find his way home. 'I'd like to help you,' that woman said, 'but, this here is the house of the Vieux Diable, and the Vieux Diable will gobble you up if he finds you here!'

'Well,' said Petit Poucet, 'I'm going to take my chances if you don't mind, that the Vieux Diable won't eat me.' He said, 'Anyway, I'd rather the Vieux Diable eat me than those bugs in the woods and to be alone in the night. I'll take my chances.'

'Well,' said the woman, 'okay, come on in.' So he went in.

The woman made supper early that night. She knew that the Vieux Diable would get home later, and she wanted the children to be in bed when he got home so that he wouldn't notice anything strange.

When supper was finished, she put the children to bed, and put a little bonnet on each of their heads. But Petit Poucet didn't have one. When the children fell asleep, he took the bonnet from one of them and put it on his own head.

Later that night, when the Vieux Diable got home, he sniffed around and said, 'Ooooeee! I smell fresh meat!'

'Oh!' said his wife, 'you're imagining things.'

'Sniff, sniff! Oh!' he said, 'no, I smell fresh meat.'

The wife said, 'Come and eat,' she said, 'supper's ready. I made some meat, and that's what you smell.'

So he went and ate his supper. After he went to bed, he wasn't satisfied. He still smelled fresh meat, and so he went and walked next to his children's beds and touched them. He saw the one who didn't have a little bonnet on, and he took that child. He thought that his child was the fresh meat he smelled, and so he killed and ate him."

At this, I sucked in a little gasp of fear. Marraine saw the fear in my eyes and chuckled a little, "Now child, everything will turn out ok, you'll see." I relaxed a little and waited for the rest of the story.

"When Petit Poucet saw the Vieux Diable eat that child, he was very afraid, as you can imagine. He saw where the Vieux Diable took off his boots and put his money. And so, when the Vieux Diable went back to bed, Petit Poucet stole the Vieux Diable's boots and his money and ran away. He put on the Vieux Diable's boots – he was very smart, you see, and he stole those boots so that the Vieux Diable couldn't chase after him -- and when he put those boots on, there must have been some magic in them, because they made him walk very very fast!

And so Petit Poucet walked and walked. Day broke, and he found a couple of the rocks he had thrown out of the wagon. 'Oh!' he said, 'Looks like I'm on the right path.' So he continued and found his house at last. He had finally come home.

And when he arrived home with the Vieux Diable's magic boots and all that money, his family was happy to see him, because now he was rich, and they were very poor. The money he brought with him made their lives much easier and so they welcomed him back and were happy with him after that."

When she finished the story, Marraine laughed and said, "you see, Tite Melee, I saved you from the Vieux Diable," and she laughed again. I laughed too, though I didn't yet understand.

After that I was always afraid that I would find the Vieux Diable whenever I went into the woods. The sound of the bullfrogs terrified me. They sounded like the deep voice of the Vieux Diable going, "Sniff, sniff, fresh meat! Sniff, sniff, fresh meat!" Sometimes I did see him, a dark figure, watching me. I never saw his face, even in my dreams, but he was always there watching me, and sometimes I would wake up and see him leaning over my bed, ready to snatch me up and eat me. When I left the safety of my Marraine and my Grandmother's homes and had to return to the little shack in the swamp, I realized that the Vieux Diable was not a monster in the woods. It was my father.

I found that in my father's house, my thoughts and feelings weren't to be shared without receiving a slap across the face or a kick in the backside, and so I learned quickly to keep them to myself. My five brothers, all wild and rough and dirty, made fun of my pretty dresses and me. I knew nothing about hunting or fishing and so to them I was worthless. I was the only girl in a house of men.

"Tite Melee," said my father soon after I had arrived, "you have to work like you're a woman now. You are the woman of the house."

And so, I worked, every day. I cooked, cleaned, and chopped wood for the fire. I worked in the garden. I washed our clothes. None of that bothered me. It was the work I had to do at night that I hated.

When I was twelve years old, my father took me into his bed for the first time. My brothers were sleeping above us in the garconniere, as usual. My screams did not awaken them. My father put his hand over my mouth. After that, it was every night. When he was finished, I would go back to my little cot and dream again that I was drowning.

Life continued like that for five more years until a preacher who was traveling in the bayous came to the little village near our house. He had a daughter, Mathilde, not very pretty, but sweet. She was twenty years old, and we became friends. She would come to my house often, and help me with my work, always chatting and laughing.

"Tite Melee," she told me, "you're so beautiful!" and she kissed me on the cheek.

One day she came to my house with bruises all over her body. She told me her father beat her and that he did it all the time. After that, Mathilde moved in with us. She slept with me in my little bed, and my father no longer took me into his bed.

Three months later, we were celebrating my eighteenth birthday together. My father and my brothers were out fishing, and Mathilde brought some wine home for us to drink. We started drinking in the morning and kept drinking until late at night, playing rock and roll records and dancing around the house in our socks. By the time my father got home, we were drunk. He didn't yell like I expected, instead he poured himself some wine and began drinking with us. He stayed up, laughing and dancing with Mathilde until long after I had crawled off to my cot to sleep. The next morning, I woke up and found her in my father's bed. It was the best present I had ever received.

After that, Mathilde changed. She would sit on my father's lap and whisper in his ear after supper. She didn't help me around the house anymore and criticized every little thing I did.

"My goodness!" she said to my father one time, "I don't know how you can stand living here. This place is such a dump, and it ain't like Melee does much to make it any better. What you need around here is a woman's touch. A REAL woman's touch."

My father said something lewd about Mathilde touching him, which made her giggle, and then he gave her sloppy wet kisses and the two of them sent me outside to the porch and locked the door. This began to happen almost every night, and I would often fall asleep out there in a rocking chair, bitten up by mosquitoes by the time the sun came up.

Her annoyance with me soon turned to anger and she would shout at me, and sometimes she would slap me. I didn't mind. I just wanted her to stay and be my friend and keep my father away from me. One day after supper, I was clearing away the dishes and she was sitting on my father's lap as usual.

"You don't love me, do you?" she pouted.

"Mais oui," my father protested, "Of course I do! How can you say that?"

"SHE's still here, isn't she?" she said jerking her head at me.

"Well, cher, where would she go? She don't have no place to go."

"I don't care!" Mathilde pouted. "I don't want her anymore, and if you want me around, then you'd better do something about it!"

It wasn't long after that, my father woke me up early in the morning,

"Get up, Melee," he said, pushing me with his foot, "get up and pack your things, we're going to Techeville today."

I didn't argue. I would only get a slap on the face for my trouble, and so I packed the few belongings that I had into a little bag and set off for the long walk to Techeville.

My father's old pick up truck had long since died. It was sitting out in the yard like an ancient ruin, its axles propped up on cinder blocks. The bumpers were orange with rust and falling off. Grass grew up through the engine and a swarm of bees had made a hive in the moldy old seats. My father's hunting dogs lolled about under the truck's carcass, sleeping and scratching at fleas. As we left, I turned and took one last look at that ramshackle house and then trudged off into the woods with my father.

A mile or so later, we found the dirt road that lead north toward Techeville. The sky had turned dark and the wind started to whip.

"Poo-yie!" my father spat on the ground. "Look like we in for a storm! I'll try to flag down a car that passes by. Maybe we can get a ride for a little bit."

But no cars came by. The road was completely deserted. The wind began to pick up even more. We passed a small farmstead, and heard a screen door banging over and over again, the wind blowing it open and closed, open and closed. After a short time, the first raindrops began to fall on us.

"Ain't no going back now, I'm afraid," said my father. He pulled his hat down around his ears and trudged on, the rain falling harder and faster as we went. It soon turned the dirt road to mud, which made our going even slower and more difficult. My father tried to say something to me from time to time, but I couldn't hear him above the pounding roar of the storm. Now and again, when lightening would flash in the sky, he would pull me under a tree on the side of the road, and we'd stay there until it seemed to pass.

The rain washed over me until it felt like I was drowning, just like in my dreams. I could barely see in front of me, and my father had to reach back and pull me along out of the mud. Now and again, one of my shoes would get sucked into the mud and be pulled off, and my father would curse and mutter as I struggled to put it back on.

I wondered what my father would do with me once we got to Techeville. Would he just leave me there? Would he give me money to get on a bus to Lafayette? I guess it didn't really matter. I would be grateful to go anywhere out of the rain. By the time we made it to Techeville, however, the town was deserted. Shops were closed and the lights were out. I began to feel a little desperate. It was suppertime and we hadn't eaten all day.

"Eh voila," said my father, pointing across the square, "there's a light still on in that drugstore. Let's go over der and see what we can see."

We walked across the square and were about to enter when my father stopped me.

"Now, Melee, I don't want you to open your mouth, you hear? You just keep quiet and let me talk. I wanna see if maybe someone here know if you can be a maid or something around here."

And that was how I came to work for Sally and Bram Palmer. I know that Miss Sally doesn't want me here, and I'm scared that Mr. Bram does. I can see it in his eyes. I know what he is thinking of me, and yet I can't keep him from thinking that way. It was the same look my father would give me, as though I was a piece of meat he wanted to devour: "fresh meat." But, like Petit Poucet, I decided to take my chances. It was better to be here than out in the night, alone.

CHAPTER NINE

I awoke to the irritating sound of heels clicking across the hard wood floor. The alarm clock had not gone off. I rolled over from my stomach to my back, allowing the sun's brightness to sear through my eyelids for a moment. I heard the whirr of the ceiling fan above me, impotent in its effort to provide anything more than a stirring of the air across my sweating face. Even if I had wanted to sleep longer, the heat of a Louisiana summer morning just would not let me.

The heel clicking grew louder, more impatient. I could tell Sally wanted me up. It was Sunday morning, and we would be late to church if I didn't hurry. Ten years of marriage with Sally and we had never missed a single Sunday mass. Mass was a numbing comfort to Sally: a place where we could be seen together as the good couple, kneeling side by side near the front of the church. The pillars of society, the Landry family, stood in the old oak pews like the columns that supported the church's arched ceiling. From where we always sat, we could just see the shining bald spot of old man Landry's head.

I pulled myself out of the damp sheets and fumbled my way to the bathroom. After a quick wash and a shave, I pulled on yet another starched shirt, pleated dress pants and tie. The same uniform I wore every day to work, in varying colors. The same clothes I'd been wearing every day for ten long years. I often envied the delivery men who wheeled dollies of supplies into the store, wiping a sweaty handkerchief across their brows and then tucking it into the pocket of their work overalls while I signed for the new shipment. Their clothes were stained and wrinkled, but comfortable --clothes that they could step out of in the evening and on the weekends to don a pair of jeans. Sundays they would feel good putting on the one dress shirt and nice pair of pants they owned. It was not a chore; it was something they might have enjoyed. There was nothing comforting to me about the suits I wore every day like the false smile that played on Sally's lips.

There was no breakfast this morning. There was a pot of coffee made, and I found a piece of the cornbread leftover from yesterday's lunch. It was sweet and moist, and I dipped a bit of it into my coffee and watched the crumbs bob up and down in my cup.

"Thanks for making the coffee, Sally," I mumbled, mouth full of cornbread.

"I didn't," she sighed, flicking through the coupons in the Sunday paper, "I guess that girl made some before she left this morning."

"Left?" I gasped. The sudden inhalation brought a suffocating swallow of bread crumbs down my windpipe. I spent an embarrassing few minutes coughing and wheezing.

"Well of course, Bram, it is Sunday, and I suppose she's gone to visit family or whatever it is she has to do." Sally muttered, annoyed with me.

I realized that it was Melee's day off, but I was surprised that she had gone. I could not imagine she'd be making the long trip back to her home only two days after she'd got here, but I did not know where else she'd go.

I continued to think about it as we drove silently to church. I parked the car, walked around to open the door for Sally, and then dragged slowly along behind her. She was the debutante again, smiling and greeting everyone as she walked up the steps and into the church.

By the time I got to our usual spot in the third pew, Sally was already seated, whispering with her mother. I had to cross over her parents to get to my place beside her. Bordelon grumbled to himself as he shifted his feet to make room. Sally was clutching her rosary in her white gloved hand. The smell of her perfume was suddenly dense and thick around my nose, tickling my throat, gagging me slightly. I pulled down the kneeler and took my place, my elbows perched on the back of the pew in front of us, pulling my hands together in prayer and resting my head against my knuckles. I closed my eyes and pretended to pray, the image of Melee's white thigh glistening in the moonlight suddenly flooding my mind. I could tell that Sally thought I was distracted, because her voice rose slightly above a whisper.

"As long as you feel alright with it, darlin'" her mother's tone was reassuring, and concerned. "If you don't like her, you know your daddy and I can find someone else for you."

"I know, Mother," sighed Sally, "I guess I'll just have to wait and see."

I worked to keep a smile from betraying me. Sally was more disturbed about Melee's presence in our home than I had anticipated. For once she was not getting exactly her way, and it was bothering her. I found that thought immensely satisfying. Sally's mother was about to say something else when the peals of the organ rang out, announcing the opening hymn. I rose to my feet and grabbed the hymnal in front of me, slightly ahead of Sally's fingers. She hesitated for a moment, and then leaned closer to her mother to share her hymnal instead. I found myself singing out louder and clearer than I had in a long time.

The fact was I didn't really need a hymnal. While my family never officially belonged to any church, my father sold bibles at nearly every revival in the South from Texas to Georgia. My sister and I would sit in the car, or on the ground outside the church or the tent, and play for hours while the fervent believers inside would sing hymn after hymn. After a while, I could tell by the songs whether it was a Baptist or Pentecostal congregation. Sometimes if we were terribly bored, or if the weather was bad, Gracie and I would sneak in to sit in the back. I often felt compelled to walk down to the front during testimony time. I would kneel in front of the minister who would anoint my head with oil and ask me if I accepted the Lord Jesus Christ as my personal lord and savior.

I thought about this question a lot as a boy. I wondered if it meant that I could have Jesus as a kind of keepsake, like the statue of St. Christopher that my father had glued to the dashboard of our car. I would always nod and say "yes," and then close my eyes to hear the "Thank you Jesus's" and "Praise the Lords" that would bubble up from the people watching me. I could picture their smiling faces and uplifted hands, and I could feel the warmth and acceptance washing over me in that moment.

After Gracie died, it was this feeling of belonging -- leaving the lonely emptiness of myself and entering into the collective mind of the congregation that I think made the experience so much like being born again. Even more satisfying were the times that I was baptized, often immediately after accepting Jesus Christ, depending on the particular revival. I would be dressed in white robes and the minister would hold his hand over my head and bless me, dipping me backward into the warm water, the buzzing sound of grief in my head silenced momentarily by the water filling my ears, and then drowned out completely by the congregation singing Now I Belong to Jesus. Once I emerged, I found that I could breathe again for a while. The heavy sadness that constricted my chest and made it so difficult to fully expand my lungs would be lifted for an afternoon. It was this release that I craved and that drove me to sneak into revival after revival, hoping to wash away the pain and the guilt. Over the years of my childhood, I was born again and baptized more than fifty times.

At the Our Lady of Sorrows Catholic church of Techeville, where Sally and I had been married and where we attended mass every Sunday, there was no such release for me. God had retreated behind the marble sculptures of Jesus, the Saints and apostles that adorned the walls and altar. The ancient priest, Father Ryan, recited mass in Latin. The inflection and tone of his voice was the same every Sunday, week to week. While I did not understand Latin, I knew when I needed to stand, sit or kneel based solely on the way his voice would rise and fall. The congregation mumbled the responses joylessly, eyes closed, retreating into the individual sanctuary of his or her own mind. I looked around at their faces and could see the peace I could not share. My mind had long ago become a place I avoided. There was no comfort in the memories and thoughts that played behind my closed eyes. Mass, like every other activity of my life, was a robotic fulfillment of expectations.

When time for the benediction finally came and went, and the priest and altar boys had led the procession out of church, I breathed a long sigh of relief. Rather than linger with Sally to greet friends and neighbors, I excused myself to smoke outside on the church steps. I was on my third cigarette when she finally appeared, linked arm in arm with Peg on one side and Junior on the other. I could see the stress on her face, and my back stiffened. Blanchard leaned over and whispered something in her ear while Peg gathered up her brood and began to shoo them down the steps. Sally glanced up and, catching my eye, shook her head once at Blanchard. He followed the direction of her gaze and, seeing me, gave a gruff nod.

"We were just talking about driving over to Grandma and Grandpa Landry's" explained Sally, her voice too shrill. This was of course, no surprise. We spent every Sunday afternoon at the Landry's.

"Mmm hmm," I mumbled, "Did you want to ride with Peg?" I asked.

"Oh no, that's alright," Sally forced a smile.

She followed me to our car, and I opened the door and helped her in. As soon as we were out of sight of her family, her face settled back into its natural state of carved granite.

The ride out to the Landry's was pleasant enough with or without Sally. It took us a few miles to the north, beyond the town limits. The homes became fewer and further between, until there was nothing but fields on either side of the road. The Landry's had sold off much of their land to small-time cotton and sweet-potato farmers. It was clear, however, when you breached the Southern border of the Landry property, because the sugar cane appeared like a wall on the horizon. Deep green and over six feet high at this time of year, the cane rose like a strange forest in this flat and marshy landscape. Planting, harvesting and processing the cane was back-breaking work. One hundred years ago, the Landrys owned more than 100 slaves to do it, as well as tending the vegetable gardens and animals, cooking the food, running the home; all the things that made the plantation a self-sufficient island in an ocean of cane.

The Landry property at one time stretched for miles -- nearly all of Canaan parish -- covered in thousands of acres of cane. People sometimes called it "Cane parish," and it was the promised land of sugar, the richest of all cash crops. But it was brutal work for the slaves, and after the civil war and emancipation, the freed people left the cane fields in a mass Exodus, and over two hundred years of miserable, grinding, sixteen-hour days in oppressive heat came to an end. Without the hands to perform the labor, the Landry's cane fields were sold off and the plantation life became a memory: some sweet and some bitter. The remaining few acres of cane were more or less symbolic now, a souvenir of the plantation's past life.

I turned the car up the private lane that led to the main house – the Grande Maison – as it was called. It was more palace than house, and at one time it must have been breathtaking. The driveway leading to it was lined with live oaks, centuries old, their thick branches dipping down to the ground, as if they were respectfully greeting us with a low bow. Rounding the corner, the Grande Maison rose majestically, its enormous Greek columns standing like silent sentinels, watching our approach.

I never got used to the sheer opulence of the place. It hinted at a depth of wealth that I could not fathom. The remaining slave shacks that crumbled in a long row behind the house were a reminder of how that wealth was achieved. For Sally, on the other hand, it was simply her grandparents' house. She did not seem to know or care about the plantation's history. For her, the tumble-down shacks were her play houses growing up. She and her sisters and cousins would play tag and hide and seek, chasing each other in and out of them, oblivious to the ghosts of families that laughed and loved, toiled and suffered, lived and died here.

I parked the car in the yard among dozens of others. Sally's mother Alice was one of seven children, each now having their own children and grandchildren. Family gatherings at the Landry plantation were huge. I was nearly knocked over by a crowd of giggling, running children, all dressed in their Sunday church clothes, racing each other across the freshly cut grass. Sally smiled wistfully at them, and then turned and trotted toward the house, eager, I assumed, to get away from me as quickly as possible and join the protective circle of her own.

I spent the afternoon as I always did – mechanically greeting those I knew and trying hard to remember everyone's names and occupations. Had I already asked this one about their new baby? Did that one buy a car last month? The mimosas that flowed like water did not help me. I concentrated on filling my mouth as much as possible with the food served for brunch: poached eggs with hollandaise, hot buttermilk biscuits, crepes, grits, spicy sausage, ham and sometimes oysters. The more I ate, the more likely I was to have a mouthful of food, and the better to shrug and smile and avoid conversations.

Sally made her rounds, her laughter pealing like silver bells and echoing in the great hall. When I'd had more than I could stand of food, champagne and polite conversation, I went searching for my wife. I saw her across the hall, again in quiet conversation with Blanchard, her head leaning close to his, her mouth puckered in a pout that she must have perfected as a little girl. He put his arm around her shoulders and pulled her closer to him. I watched as he inhaled the scent of her hair, closed his eyes and kissed her forehead. Sally noticed me, and instantly moved a quick step away from him. Turning to find the source of the interruption, he glared at me with narrowed eyes.

"Ready to go, Sally?" I grinned, knowing how annoyed Blanchard must be with me at that moment.

"What?" protested Blanchard. "You can't be wanting to leave so soon."

"Yes, in fact I do," I insisted. "I'm quite tired and I'd like to get a nap in before the day's out, to tell you the truth."

I saw Sally bite her lip, her cheeks flushing at my lack of couth. I relished the thought that I was embarrassing her.

"I'll wait for you in the car," I announced, giving her a little tap on her behind for good measure, and smiled as the redness in her cheeks deepened.

It wasn't long before Sally joined me, her mouth drawn in a tight line. I knew she was furious and too humiliated to stay. I didn't care. I didn't even open the door for her. She stood waiting for a moment outside the car, and then sighed and let herself in as I adjusted the volume of the radio. We rode home as we always did – in complete silence.

As soon as we reached the house, Sally jumped from the car, slamming the door as hard as she could, and stalked off to the house. I took my time, strolling around the garage, thinking I might smoke a cigarette before going in. I was surprised to find Melee and Gabriel behind the garage. Melee was smiling, leaning against the wall, and Gabriel stood next to her, holding his bike at his side.

"Gabe," I stammered, confused, "didn't expect to see you here today, don't you ever take a day off?" The friendliness in my voice was forced. There was something a little too familiar about the way he was smiling at Melee.

"Oh, no sir, I mean yes sir," Gabriel stuttered, surprised to see me.

Melee giggled, not at all disturbed by my presence and clearly comfortable with Gabriel.

"I was just . . . in the neighborhood . . . and thought I'd stop by to say hello," he continued, staring at his feet and rubbing his neck.

"Well, now, that'd be a first." I said in a low voice. In the five years Gabriel had worked for me, he'd never been around on a Sunday.

"I'd best be getting home," he said, throwing his leg over the bicycle. "See you tomorrow, Mr. Bram. Goodbye Miss Melee," he kicked the bike into motion and was gone.

Melee watched him go, and then turned and gave me a smile. It instantly washed away any misgivings I had. Her smile was intoxicating, affecting me far more than the mimosas I had consumed earlier in the day.

"Did you have a nice day off?" I asked, and instantly felt like an idiot.

"Yes, it was fine," she smiled again, seeming amused by my question and obvious embarrassment. There was something different in the way that she looked at me. She was more easy and relaxed, as if she was becoming more comfortable here.

I was racking my brain for another bit of small talk that I could throw her way to keep a conversation going, but I couldn't find any words. Instead I just stood there, staring at her with my mouth open. She waited patiently for me to speak, and then gave up.

"Well, Mr. Bram, I think I'll go in now, if you don't mind."

"Oh, yeah, sure, sure," I stuttered, again feeling ridiculous.

I watched her go inside, and then cursed myself. Why were my hands shaking? Why was it so difficult to talk to her? I knew the answer before I asked myself. It was because I didn't want to talk to her. I wanted to hold her – to pull her near me and breathe in the scent of her, bury my face in her dark hair, feel the warmth of her body pressed tightly to mine, unbutton her blouse and free her soft breasts, crush my mouth against her and taste her. The thoughts came faster and faster, my fantasy growing more real and unsettling, and my desire becoming more unbearable by the second. I leaned back against the garage, trying to calm myself, and caught a faint whiff of her that remained. I was feeling something I never had before. It was a passion that I thought was lost to me, and that I would never experience. It was both agony and rapture, bliss and torture. It was more moving than any religious experience. It was the feeling that whatever happened from now until the end of my life, I would never be the same, and I would always find myself pulled toward her, revolving around her like the moth to the light.

I spent most of the evening outside, smoking cigarettes, straightening the tool shed, anything I could do to distract myself and delay going in. Sally never came out to find me. I guessed that she had taken her pills again and was in a deep sleep. The light in our bedroom turned off shortly after dark. Once I was sure that she had turned in, I crept my way into the house.

It was almost painful to put myself into the bed with Sally. I could feel the chill radiating from her body. It made me shudder. Even in sleep I could sense the tension and anger she was keeping. I could feel how she was perched on the edge of the bed, as far away from me as possible. I followed suit, covering myself with the sheet and turning away from her, I clung to the edge of the bed, gritted my teeth, and screwed my eyes shut, hoping sleep would come quickly.

At that moment, I heard a creaking in the ceiling above me. Melee was walking around in her room. I listened to the sound of her feet shuffling across the floor, and thought I might have heard her sigh. I felt my body relaxing as I thought of her, and drifted back into my fantasies. I fell asleep thinking about Melee and I lying together between a row of sugar cane, the shade of the tall green stalks protecting us from the summer heat, the coolness of the earth beneath us and Melee's sighs ringing in my ears.

CHAPTER TEN

Monday morning dawned, and I woke to a feeling of anticipation. Melee had only been with us for a little more than two days, and already so much had changed. I found myself whistling as I washed and shaved, listening to the bacon sizzle in the kitchen and knowing that I would see her in only a few minutes. Sally had already dressed and gone outside to work in her garden. The French doors from our room to the private back porch were open, and I could feel a breeze flowing through as I dressed. It was cooler, less humid than the weekend had been, strange for the end of July. As I stood in front of the mirror adjusting my tie, I heard mumbled voices from outside. It was Sally and what sounded like two men speaking, but I couldn't hear what they were saying. I hurried to finish dressing and see who it was, when there came a loud rap at the back door. Who would be knocking this early and why wouldn't Sally have let them in?

I was fumbling to buckle my belt when I heard the kitchen door open. Melee must have answered it.

"Melee Mouton?" boomed a man's voice.

"Yes." I barely heard her response.

"You're under arrest for theft. You have the right to remain silent. . ."

I felt the blood rush from my face as I clambered out of the bedroom and into the kitchen. Sheriff Boyle was placing Melee in handcuffs while reading her rights. She turned and stared at me, her face full of panic and shock.

"What's this all about?" I shouted.

"Good morning, Bram," said Blanchard, stepping into the kitchen behind Boyle. "Don't worry now, we just have a little matter that we need to talk to your employee about."

"A little matter? You're arresting her!" I shouted again. The smug expression on Blanchard's face was infuriating.

"Like I said, this doesn't concern you," Blanchard continued, "we have reason to believe that Ms. Mouton's been involved in a robbery and we need to take her in for questioning."

"The hell you do!" I growled back. I could feel my face turning red, the anger and panic making my stomach churn. I was shaking, my hands clenching into fists, trying to hold myself back from pushing the sheriff away from Melee. Suddenly he looked up at me with a forced smile.

"Bram, you better back off, now!" he warned, patting his holster. "This don't involve you and you should just stay out of it."

I stood helpless, watching Boyle lead Melee out by her elbow, her arms pulled behind her back in handcuffs, her head lowered in humiliation. She was wearing the ridiculous maid's uniform that Sally had insisted on. It was much too big for her tiny frame and made her look like a little girl.

Boyle led Melee out to his car and put her in the back seat. Blanchard tipped his hat at Sally, who was kneeling down on the ground, pulling weeds. She glanced up at him quickly and nodded, then returned to her work. Blanchard shot me another smug glance, and I seethed as a slight smile spread on the corner of his lips. He let himself in the passenger's side and then Boyle tore off toward town.

I watched them go, and then stood trembling in fury at the top of the steps. It took me a moment to realize how strange it was that Sally was so calm -- too calm.

"You knew about this, didn't you!" I hissed through my teeth.

"Don't know what you're talking about," Sally answered, clearly trying to avoid meeting my eyes.

"Like hell!" I growled. At that moment a cannon went off inside me. Everything after that happened very fast. With three quick leaps I bounded down the steps and grabbed a fist full of Sally's hair. She screamed and then covered her mouth with her hands.

"Goddammit, Sally, this time you've gone too far!" I bellowed.

I pulled her by the hair back up the steps, through the kitchen and into our bedroom and threw her down on the floor next to the bed. She was panting, trying desperately to keep from screaming again, to keep the neighbors from hearing us.

"Bram, what are you doing?!" she gasped. She looked up at me with tears streaking her face, the mascara running down in rivers toward her mouth. I honestly couldn't answer her question. I had never struck Sally -- never even raised my voice to her -- but at that moment I wasn't in control of my body. It was controlling me.

I walked around the room, shutting the windows and pulling the curtains closed. I shut and locked the French doors, and then I returned to Sally. I slapped her hard across the face and then picked her up and threw her face down on the bed. Now she was really sobbing. I jerked her arm up behind her and placed my knee on her back, leaning over to whisper in her ear.

"You just couldn't stand not having your way, could you?" I spit. "Could you?!"

She whimpered unintelligibly into the quilt.

"Had to get your old boyfriend involved, huh? It isn't enough that you've made me miserable in every way possible, is it, Sally? Now you have to try to humiliate me in front of those two goons. What did you do? What did you tell them to make them come here?" I was shouting again.

She didn't answer. Instead she began wailing, her cries muffled by the quilt. I threw her onto her back and straddled her. Pulling her arms above her head, I screamed into her face.

"Answer me!"

Sally was really frightened now. Her eyes stared at me in horror.

"I, I told them I thought Melee had stolen that necklace from M-Meyer's," she stuttered.

I stared at her, my mouth opening, trying to process what she had said.

"What? Why?" I yelled. "How could you?!"

"Sh-she had a s-silver necklace on," she choked out, "it was like what Warren had described."

"So you decided to turn her in, did you?" I glared at her. "Went to Daddy and pouted about it. Asked good ol' Blanchard if he could come riding in his shiny armor and rescue you, huh? God, you make me sick!" I pushed myself off her and walked a few steps back from the bed.

"You'd better be wrong, Sally," I snarled, "because if anything happens to that girl, I will slap that pout off your face – permanently!"

I marched over to my dresser and grabbed the car keys. Sally sat up on the bed, wiping her face with the back of her hand.

"Wh-where are you going?" she whimpered.

"To town, Sally. To see what I can do about this mess you've made. I'm leaving and you're staying right here, you hear me? You stay right here in this room and don't you step foot out of it! If I find out you've left this room, or called your momma, you will be sorry!"

I was yelling at the top of my lungs, shot one last glance at Sally's tear-streaked face, and then slammed the door behind me. The force rattled the walls. I sailed through the kitchen out the back door, jumped into my car and was on the road to town in less than a minute.

As I drove, my feelings flashed between rage and terror. The panic seemed to be boiling through my veins, burning my lungs, raging through my head. The blood pounded in my ears, drowning out the sound of my car's engine as I roared into town. I slowed down as I neared the main square, and pulled my car in behind the sheriff's cruiser, parked across the street from the drugstore, in front of Meyer's Jewelers.

I jumped out of my car, and stood panting for a moment, trying to regain my composure before I entered the store. It was still early – not even nine o'clock yet. Meyer's would not open until ten, but Blanchard and the sheriff were inside, talking to Ira. I pulled out my handkerchief from my pocket and wiped the sweat that was pouring off my head and down the back of my neck, then I pushed the door open and walked in.

"Bram! Welcome!" beamed Ira. I was surprised to see him so cheerful. "Please, join us, we were just talking to your lovely new house guest."

Ira, always kind and warm, seemed angelic, a halo of white hair floated above his balding head. He was standing behind the display case, his elbows propped up on the glass countertop. He peered at me through the round spectacles perched at the end of his nose. To his right stood Blanchard, leaning against the counter with his left elbow. On the opposite stood Melee, her head still slightly bowed. Boyle had removed her handcuffs, but was still holding her elbow. Seeing him standing so near her made my stomach lurch again.

Blanchard eyed me with distaste. "Well, Bram, true to form, you continue to meddle in things that don't concern you. I declare, I don't think I've seen a man so interested in the domestic help in all my life," he snickered and Boyle smiled, shaking his head.

I froze in my steps. Could Blanchard read me that well? I hoped that he did not have a deeper meaning behind his comment. Ira perceived my uneasiness and, always the good host, attempted to make me comfortable.

"Do come in, Bram," he smiled. "Now gentlemen," he turned to Blanchard, "what can I do for you this morning?"

Blanchard cleared his throat and straightened up to his full height, taking the posture he usually had in front of the jury in court.

"Ira, we believe that we may have caught the person who took that necklace from here on Friday night,"

"Oh?" responded Ira. He also stood up straight, folding his hands in front of him.

"Show him the necklace," prompted Boyle, giving Melee a nudge with his elbow.

Melee slowly turned her face toward me. I could see the fear rising. Her eyes were tearing up and she was struggling to stay calm. She reached up behind her neck with shaking hands and slowly unclasped the silver chain around her neck. Holding the pendant gently in one hand and the chain in the other, she placed the necklace on the counter.

Ira hummed. "Interesting." He pulled his magnifying glass from a drawer and bent over to examine the necklace more closely. After a few long minutes, he stood back up, a wide smile on his face.

"It's a beautiful necklace, that's for certain, but it isn't the one that was stolen from here."

Blanchard and Boyle both stiffened with surprise. I felt my knees begin to give way from relief.

"Are you sure about that Ira?" accused Boyle, "It is Saint Anne on there, right?"

"Yes, yes indeed," agreed Ira. "But the necklace that was stolen was platinum. This is sterling silver. Lovely and durable, but not platinum. Also the inscription. The pendant that was stolen had 'Saint Anne, Pray for Us,' written in English. This has an inscription in French. I'm afraid I don't speak French so I'm not sure what it says," he smiled again, and then handed the necklace back to Melee.

"Where did you get such a pretty necklace?" Ira asked Melee. She was fumbling again with the clasp, trying to place the necklace back around her neck.

"My mother," answered Melee, her head raising just a little, "when she died."

"Well that was a beautiful gift," said Ira. He smiled kindly at her and then turned to Blanchard.

"So, Mr. Blanchard, I'm afraid we have not yet caught the thief. Perhaps we should let Bram take the girl home now. I'm sure she's had a difficult morning."

Blanchard scowled over Melee's head at Boyle, and then squeezed his eyes shut.

"Alright," he sighed. "Sorry to trouble you this morning, Miss Melee, you're free to go."

Melee nodded and then walked toward me. I held the door open for her, and tossed a glare back at Blanchard and Boyle.

"I'd appreciate it if you refrain from invading my home again, gentlemen," I grumbled. "Ira, thank you kindly." I gave him a quick smile and then followed Melee out.

She walked like a ghost, floating along and staring vacantly. I began to worry, wondering what she was thinking. Would she leave now? I would not blame her. I hurried to open the car door for her and helped her inside. She averted her eyes from me as she slipped into the front seat, folding her hands in her lap and bowing her head.

I started up the car, and then began a slow drive out of town. Melee was silent. I was screaming in my head, wondering what I could say to comfort her. I didn't want to drive back to my house, thinking that seeing Sally would just upset Melee more, but I didn't exactly know where to go, so I drove east, crossing over the Bayou Teche bridge and heading out on the winding road toward New Orleans.

After about twenty minutes of driving, the landscape turned marshy, murky swamp water stretching out on either side of the road. The cypress trees laden with Spanish moss shaded the car from the sun's glare. We drove on the raised road over the swamp and then emerged into rice country. I pulled off the road onto a gravel drive and parked under a massive oak tree. A squirrel chattered overhead.

"Melee, I'm so sorry," I broke the silence, "I . . . I don't know what to say." She didn't answer.

"Would you like for me to take you home? I mean, back to your father's house?"

Her eyes darted at me quickly, full of shock and fear. Her face suddenly crumpled up, and she began to cry.

"You don't want me anymore?" she sobbed, covering her face with her hands.

"No, no, that's not what I meant!"

I turned my body toward her, my hands shaking, I rested my arm on the back of the seat and inched closer to her. She glanced at me, agony in her face.

"Please don't send me back dere. I can't go back. I can never go back!" she pleaded.

"You don't have to! You don't ever have to. Melee, I promise you, I will never let anything hurt you again." My hand moved toward her and slowly, softly rested on her back.

With a heavy sigh, she leaned toward me, and I closed the space between us, wrapping my arms around her and pulling her toward me. She didn't resist. Instead, she buried her face into my chest, soaking my shirt with her tears. I held her close to me for a long while, stroking her back and running my fingertips through her black hair. I could smell her hair – feel its silky smoothness. I leaned forward and kissed the top of her head.

She looked up at me, and I pulled back, worried that I had gone too far, but her eyes were soft, a tear clinging to the end of her long lashes. She seemed to be waiting for me. I gently placed my hands on the sides of her face, brushing the tears away with my thumbs. She sighed, and leaning her head back, closed her eyes – and then my lips were on hers.

She didn't pull away. Her lips responded to mine, pulling me into her. I felt her wrapping her arms around my neck, her mouth opening to the pressure of my tongue. I gave in to my hunger for her, kissing her mouth, the edge of her jaw, her neck. Her breath came in soft gasps and she twined her fingers into my hair.

At the sound of a car coming down the road, she pushed me away and scooted back over the seat. I turned and gripped the steering wheel, willing my breath to calm down, trying to clear my head of the rush of blood. For a moment I was blinded, as if I'd stared at the sun too long.

I looked in my side mirror and saw a truck moving toward us. It slowed down as it neared my car and came to a stop at the edge of a road. An old man in a straw hat leaned across his passenger seat and shouted to us through the open window.

"You folks alright?" he asked, eyeing me, and then glancing across me at Melee.

"Yes," I smiled. "Just fine, thank you."

"Something wrong with your car?" he persisted, "I got some tools in the back here if you need some help."

"Oh no, it's fine. I uh, I just wanted to check the radiator. It's a hot day." I smiled again, popped the hood, and stepped out of the car, acting out the charade for the man.

He watched me lift the hood and poke around at the radiator cap.

"You'll want to use a rag on that," he advised, "it's bound to be hot."

"Yes, thank you," I answered, pulling my handkerchief out of my pocket.

The man did not leave until I had pulled the cap off the radiator and assured him all was well.

"Alright then," he threw his gear shift into drive and revved the truck's engine, "you have a pleasant day, sir," he nodded in my direction, and then turned to Melee, "you too ma'am."

"Thank you!" I waved, then closed the hood as he drove away.

I pulled myself back behind the wheel, and tried to smile at Melee. "Guess we'd better head home." She nodded, but didn't answer.

I drove the speed limit back to the house, trying to focus on the road, though my eyes kept glancing toward Melee. She was leaning out the window, her hair whipping against her face so that I couldn't see it. I wondered again if I had gone too far and if I should say anything. When we got back to the house, Melee ran inside. I followed her, but she had already disappeared upstairs. I then remembered Sally and trudged toward our bedroom.

She was sitting at her vanity, putting make up on her face. She had already re-done her eyes. There was no trace of the mascara on her cheeks, but there was a shiny red mark where I had slapped her. The thought of it made me shudder. I watched as she covered it with foundation and then dusted her face with powder.

"Sally," I began, waiting for her to turn to me.

She ignored me, and picked up her hairbrush.

"Sally, look at me," I said louder.

Her back stiffened at the tone of my voice, and she turned around. Her eyes were narrowed and her chin raised defiantly. Her lips were drawn in a tight line across her face. I was sure that she expected an apology. The thought made my anger swell again into my throat.

"Sally," I said again, trying to keep my rage controlled. "Your attempts to remove Melee from this house have failed."

Her mouth opened in surprise for a second, but she quickly recovered.

"Melee did not steal that necklace from Meyer's. Ira Meyer himself verified that it was not the same necklace." I paused for a moment, letting that sink in.

"Now that you've gotten your little tantrum out of your system, let me make something clear," I continued, my voice hard. "You are never to question me again. You are never to defy me or embarrass me in front of your family."

She rolled her eyes and attempted to turn back toward the mirror, raising her brush up to her hair. In two short steps I was behind her. I jerked the brush out of her hand, threw it against the wall, and yanked her shoulders around to look at me. Terror welled up into her face again, and she shrank back into her chair.

"Sally, if you ever do, I will divorce you. Do you hear me? I will divorce you. I don't care about your family's money. I don't give a damn about what folks will say. I'm disgusted that I let myself be a slave to you and your father all these years, and for what? Because I felt guilty? Because I felt sorry for you? It certainly wasn't because I loved you."

Her lips quivered and I could see the tears filling her eyes again.

"You are a spoiled little girl who has grown up into a selfish and petty shrew. If you want to spend your days as a shriveled up old spinster, that's fine by me, you can leave now and going crying back to your daddy, but all the money in the world won't find you another man, Sally. You'll spend the rest of you life a lonely divorcee, living off the charity of your parents. Your friends will pity you, but they'll also be suspicious of you, wondering if they can trust their husbands around you."

She was crying now, the truth of my words sinking in.

"Bram, please," she whispered, her hands reaching toward me in supplication. I pushed them away.

"I have never asked you for anything Sally -- nothing for myself. But this time you will give me what I want, and I want Melee. I want her more than anyone or anything, do you understand? You will let me have her, and you will keep your mouth shut and that fake smile on your face for as long as I tell you to, or you can pack your things and get the hell out."

She nodded, covering her face with her hands and sobbing. She knew I was right. She couldn't bear the public shame if I rejected her. She would rather stay with me under these cruel circumstances than face a lifetime of disgrace.

I had won. Finally and unequivocally, I had won.

CHAPTER ELEVEN

I did not go in to the store that day, nor the next. I called Sally's father and told him that Sally was ill, and that I would be staying home to care for her.

"What's wrong?" he asked, "Did you call Doc Collins?"

"No Charlie, I don't think that would help her."

"Why not? What's going on?" I could hear the impatience in his voice.

"Charlie I'd rather not go into it, but Sally's been feeling. . .melancholy about some things lately. I think it would do her good to get away from here for a day. I'm thinking of taking her on a drive to Lafayette tomorrow, maybe let her do some shopping or see a picture show. I think she'll feel better with a change of scenery."

"I see," he mumbled, his tone getting softer, "well, uh, please tell her I hope she feels better, and to call us if she needs anything."

"Mmm hmm, will do," I responded.

"I guess I'll see you Wednesday?" he asked.

"Yes sir, bright and early." I hung up the phone.

The ruse I had created wasn't so far from the truth. Sally was immediately stricken with a migraine and took to her bed for the next three days. I spent my time in Melee's room. That first afternoon, I waited in the kitchen for her, trying to give her some time to recover from the frightening events of the morning. I was giddy. Disbelieving what I had done, and amazed at how easy it had been to conquer Sally. I wondered why I hadn't done it before. There was only one thing missing to secure my happiness, and that was Melee. Would she still want me? Did she regret what had happened in my car that morning?

I finally could wait no longer, and climbed the stairs to the garconniere, my heart beating faster with every step. Her door was shut. I shuffled quietly through the maze of junk in the attic, and knocked softly. There was no answer. I knocked again and waited. There was no sound from within. After what seemed like an eternity, I tried the door knob, it was not locked so I pushed the door open and let myself in.

Melee was sitting on the edge of her bed with her back to me, staring out the window. She did not stir when I came in. She seemed to still be in the same trance as she was when she left Meyer's store.

"Melee?" I whispered, hoping that she wouldn't mind my presence. She still did not move, and so I carefully made my way around the bed. I hesitated for a moment, and then reached out to touch her shoulder.

She suddenly came to life, turning toward me she clutched my hand in hers and kissed it. The feel of her lips on my flesh made my knees buckle. I pulled her up and wrapped my arms around her waist, kissing her forehead, her eyes, her cheeks. My lips travelled down until I found her mouth and then I was kissing her hungrily, feeling her body pressed tightly against me. I gently lowered her to the bed and raised my head to look at her. She still did not speak, but she looked into my eyes. There was longing and trust in them. I did not know how I could possibly deserve this, but I didn't care. She was so young, so very young, and yet she had a knowing about her, an old soul. Instead of the shy fumbling of a school girl, she met my desire in equal measure, pulling me into her, seeming to need me as much as I needed her and never seeming to get enough.

Those first days passed in a blur. I was surprised when Wednesday finally dawned, although I did not rush to get to the store. I spent the next few weeks and months living life as I pleased. I came and went at the store as I wanted. Bordelon attempted to reprimand me for my casualness at first, but I scoffed at him.

"You can fire me if you want, Charlie, but where would that leave dear Sally?" I laughed.

He glared at me, but seemed to know I was right. I would need to at least have the appearance of working for a living for Sally's sake. It would be humiliating for her to be seen with a shiftless husband.

I found that keeping up with appearances was an effective weapon against nearly everyone in Sally's circle. We continued to be seen at parties and functions, and Sally's persona did not alter. She was still the aging debutante, smiling her way around the room, her silvery laughter tinkling in the air. I began to enjoy these events, no longer feeling a need to impress anyone. When I was ready to leave, Sally would follow me like an obedient puppy, and no one even raised an eyebrow.

At home, Sally would disappear into our bedroom with a bottle of bourbon or vodka and a fist full of pills. She slept through her days, only stopping occasionally to eat the food that Melee brought to her on a tray. Despite Sally's resentment, Melee was respectful and kind. I adored her selflessness, so different from Sally, so beautiful to see.

My nights were filled with Melee. It seemed there were never enough hours to satisfy my need for her. Sometimes late into the night when she fell asleep on my chest, I would hold her, wondering how this strange, magical creature came into my life. Although we had spent countless hours together, I still did not really know her. When I tried to ask her, she would only smile at me, putting a finger on my lips and then kissing me. It was enough to distract me again, and I would forget my questions, her face filling my mind and crowding out all other thoughts. Still, I could not help but marvel at it all. Why would she choose me? What could possibly have been in her past that would make a future with me so appealing to her?

These thoughts wandered through my head every moment that I was away from her. I couldn't help but fear that one day she simply would not be there when I returned home, having vanished as mysteriously as she had appeared. I was puzzling over this one day at the store, wiping down the lunch counter, listening to the usual banter of the customers. I was interrupted by the sound of a familiar voice.

"Mr. Bram," I glanced up to see Annie Johnson standing across the counter from me.

"Ah, Annie, how are you?" I was surprised. She was nearly always at the Blanchard's house during the day.

"I'm fine, Mr. Bram," I noticed she was holding her hand up to her face in a strange way.

"Are you sure everything's alright?" I asked.

"Yes sir. It's Ms. Peg, she sent me her to get her some antacid. She's got heartburn something powerful."

I nodded. Peg was due to deliver any day. She had not been seen in public for the past month, waiting for the baby to arrive.

"Well, sure," I smiled. "I guess that means the baby will be a boy, right?" I asked.

"Mmm hmm, that's right, sir." She answered, distracted. I went and got the antacid for her. When I returned, I stopped in my tracks. Her arm was at her side and I saw that she had an enormous black eye.

"My God, Annie!" I exclaimed. "What happened to you?"

"Nothin' sir, nothin' at all." She held her hands out for the bottle of medicine, ducking her head down and away from my gaze.

"Can you put this on the Blanchard's credit?"

"Yes, certainly," I answered, still stunned by the sight of her swollen eye. I noticed that there was also a crusted scab on her lip, as though she had been hit there too, and a slight bruising on her neck.

"Thank you sir," she murmured, and then quickly left.

I returned to the lunch counter feeling anxious and confused. For the first time ever I was actually glad to see Blanchard and Sheriff Boyle come in at their usual time. I had not really spoken to them since Melee's arrest and that had been more than two months ago. There were of course, the awkward times when Sally and I were thrown together with Peg and Junior at various parties and the weekly bridge game, but I took advantage of the fact that Blanchard rarely had occasion to speak to me and enjoyed the silence.

This was why Blanchard was so shocked when I confronted him soon after he took his seat.

"What's happened to Annie?" I demanded.

He eyed me up, suspicious as usual. I saw Boyle's jaw muscles flex.

"Well now Bram," he began, sarcasm oozing from his voice, "worried about the domestic help again, I see."

"Come on, Junior," I grumbled, "you know I wouldn't speak to you unless it were absolutely necessary. What's happened to her?"

Blanchard took a long sip of his lemonade, licked his upper lip, and then shot a quick glance at Boyle.

"Sheriff, I guess you'd better explain this one."

Boyle shifted uncomfortably on his stool. He leaned forward and motioned me to come closer to him.

"Annie's husband, Vernon, has been lurking around lately. I guess he must've messed her up a few nights ago. Annie won't talk about it, but it seems that's what's going on." Boyle pushed himself back into his chair and then crammed a large bite of sandwich into his mouth.

"It's a shame," sighed Blanchard, shaking his head, "Peg was pretty upset by it. Last thing we want is to have some crazy nigger loitering around our house, but it seems like that's a possibility. He followed Annie home the other night."

"What?" I gasped. "Followed her home?"

"Yep, beat her up and left her on the side of the road," Blanchard shook his head.

"Jesus." I mumbled, stunned.

I turned to Boyle who was shoving another enormous bite into his mouth.

"Are you going to do anything about this?" I asked.

"Do?" he choked out, his mouth full of sandwich.

"Yeah, DO," I hissed, "you know, serve and protect and all that."

"Good God, Palmer, you have a heightened sense of morality, don't you?" laughed Blanchard.

"I do my best to stay out of the coloreds' affairs." Boyle added. "But, since Annie works for the Blanchards and they don't want Vernon Johnson coming around their place, I've been picking her up after work and driving her home, you know, just to make sure."

"And it's awful kind of you," said Blanchard, "you know if it was up to me, I'd just let Annie go, but Peg wouldn't have it. Course, I know better than to get involved with that kind of thing," he smirked and shot a knowing glance at the sheriff. I saw a slight smile forming at the corners of Boyle's mouth. I knew from this remark that the two of them still thought my keeping Melee around was a tremendous joke.

"Well, that is decent of you," I admitted to Boyle.

"Uh, yeah, all the same, Palmer, be on the lookout for him, got it? I mean, I think he's wandering around here, and if that's the case, we all had better be careful. No telling what he might do, you know." Boyle sat back and began picking his teeth with the nail on his pinky finger. I nodded and then went back to wiping down the counter.

Later in the day, after the lunch counter had closed I cornered Izzy who had come by to make the afternoon deliveries.

"Izzy, how is your mother?" I asked. He shot an anxious look at me, the smile draining immediately from his face.

"Uh, she, she alright, sir," he mumbled, ducking his head to examine his shoes.

"Izzy, you know you can tell me if something's wrong, don't you?" I said.

"Mmm hmm."

"Izzy? Israel Johnson!" I demanded, getting his attention.

"Yes sir?"

"Has your daddy been around again?" I asked, softer this time.

Izzy seemed confused, began to shake his head, and then stared back at his feet.

"I guess so, sir," he sighed.

"Well have you seen him?" I asked.

"No sir."

"Well, did he hit your mother?"

"I guess so, sir," he repeated.

"Izzy, the next time you see your daddy, I want you to come get me, you here? You come get me, and I'll do whatever I can to help your momma, alright?"

"Mmm hmm, I mean, yes sir."

Izzy kept his head ducked, so I gave him a quick pat on the shoulder, and then sent him out to make the deliveries. The afternoon went by quickly. It was the week before Halloween, and children would come after school each day to try on masks and all the costumes we sold. A woman came in with a little girl who was determined to be a witch, no matter how her mother tried to convince her to be a princess or a fairy.

"No momma! The witch! I wanna be a witch!" she pouted, her head shaking with exasperation.

Her mother eventually gave in, and the little girl insisted on wearing the witch's hat out of the store, her long curls bobbing underneath the wide black brim as she skipped along.

Before I left for the day, I put two large bottles of sleeping pills and a can of white paint in my pockets. The pills were for Sally, of course. It helped her get through the days and nights without hearing me and Melee. It was the least I could do to keep her in supply. Each evening I would put two pills on her nightstand and two more in the morning. She spent her days in bed, barely speaking. Melee continued to tend to her, bringing her food, sometimes even feeding her, giving her sponge baths and caring for her like a dedicated nurse. Sally did not complain. In fact she seemed to have formed a strange attachment to the girl, which I did not question. I only cared that Melee would be waiting for me at night after Sally dozed off.

The white paint was for my annual pilgrimage to the cemetery. Every year, before All Soul's Day, I would drive out to the cemetery beyond the town limits and spend a few hours tending to the grave of our lost child. Other relatives of lost ones would do the same, trimming the grass, cleaning and painting the tombstones. I knew the drive well, though I only went there once a year. Up the oak-lined gravel lane, through the main gates, the road wandered around to the left. I parked the car and walked North, passing the rows of Landrys, Martins and Naquins, and came to a small white marker, the lonely resting place of the only Palmer who would be buried there until her mother and father joined her.

I took out the white paint, a brush, and a clean cotton rag. I wiped down the stone, trying to remove some of the grime from the last year of neglect.

She would have been seven years old. Just a little older than Gracie was when she died. I wondered what she would look like. Would she have curly hair like Gracie did? Would she want to be a witch or a princess for Halloween? I brushed a coat of white paint carefully over the gravestone, dipping it into the P, the A, the L, lingering over the M, wondering what we would have named her. . .Pamela, Alice, Lucy, Maggie, Emily, Rachel. . .

By the time I had finished, it was getting dark and the air was chilly. I shivered and pulled my jacket up around my neck, jamming my hat down over my ears and tucking my head down. I shoved my fists into my pockets, gripping the bottles of sleeping pills in one hand and the empty paint can in the other. In seven years, Sally had not once gone to see the grave of her child. I wondered if she ever would and felt sad for the little lost soul.

"I'm sorry," I said under my breath, not knowing exactly to whom I said it.

The wind was starting to kick up when my car hit the main road back to town. I rolled my windows up and fumbled with the stereo, hoping to find a cheerful tune. A few drops of rain splattered across the windshield, and I sighed. There wasn't too much of a fall season in Louisiana. Summer seemed to last forever, with warm weather all the way into December at times, a brief period of frost through January, and then warm again as early as February. By May, it was summer. Leaves did not usually turn the glorious colors they did elsewhere in autumn, and their stay was short-lived, a hard rain in October or November would knock them all out of the trees. I felt that this was going to be another one of those fall-ending rains.

By the time I pulled into the driveway at my house it was pounding down on the car, heavy raindrops, so large it was almost possible to see them falling individually. The car's headlights were muffled by the deluge. I could barely see to pull into the garage. I ran the short distance from the car to the back porch and stood shaking, cold and wet. It wasn't until I reached for the door handle that I noticed Melee sitting in the rocking chair.

She was rocking slowly, her feet drawn up and her arms wrapped tightly around her knees. She was staring vacantly out into the night. The same vacant stare she had when I first saw her, the same stare as when I drove her away from Meyer's store after the arrest. The same stare as a person whose soul had been emptied, her eyes black and lifeless.

"Melee?" I whispered, "is everything alright?"

Without looking at me, and in a voice so low it was barely audible she murmured,

"I have seen the devil again tonight."

CHAPTER TWELVE

I've seen the Vieux Diable again, awake and in my dreams. At first I thought it was as it always has been, just my imagination -- the frightened nightmares of my childhood coming back to revisit me -- but now I am sure it is not. This time, he is there, watching me from the back yard, just out of reach of the porch light, a dark figure, unmoving, his face obscured in the night.

The first time I saw him I was taking care of Sally. I was bringing her soup that I'd made, and I fed it to her. She only eats for me now. Though I know she once hated me, now she calls for me, and I help her. I bathe her and bring her roses cut from her garden. I sit at her bedside and I tell her stories – happy ones – about Compere Lapin and Compere Bouki, and I sing to her a little. Bram does not know. He is often so cruel to her, and it frightens me, though I cannot tell him this. He comes to me every night and I give him what he wants, so that I may stay here, so that I don't have to go back to my father.

After I fed Sally the soup that night, she told me she was hot and asked me to open the windows and the door to the back porch so that she could breathe easier. As I peered out into the night I saw him, leaning against the garage. Bram was not home; he was working late at the drugstore. I stifled a scream so that he wouldn't know I was there. I stood watching him for quite a while, and he didn't move. So I shut the back door again and returned to Sally.

"Melee," she called, "are you there?"

"Yes, ma'am," I assured her.

"Don't leave me tonight until Bram comes home, please."

"Of course, ma'am."

"Melee, tell me a story. I have such a headache and your stories always make me feel better."

I sat next to her and prepared myself to tell a story, wondering which one of Marraine's collection I should tell her tonight, and then a thought came to me.

"Miss Sally, may I ask you something?" I said, stroking her hair.

"Hmm?" she mumbled.

"Why are you so sad?"

She didn't speak for a moment, and then she closed her eyes and sighed.

"Because I am lonely."

"For Mr. Bram?" I asked.

"No," she answered, and then after a long pause, "for my child. She died."

"Oh, I am sorry," I said.

And so I told her the story Marraine had given me, so long ago, about the mother who had lost a child and the child's candle, and how the mother had to let the child go. And I think that this soothed her, because her face smoothed out and she began to breathe deeply and for the first time in many weeks, she fell asleep without crying and without taking any pills.

The next morning, she woke up and sat up in bed and called me.

"Melee!" she said.

"Yes, ma'am," I answered.

"Bring me my clothes. I think I would like to work in the garden today."

And so I helped her dress, and she did work in the garden all morning, and I heard her humming from time to time. And when it was time for lunch she ate out on her back porch instead of in her bed, as usual. I waited until Bram had eaten his lunch and then he wanted to take me upstairs to my bedroom, and I gave him what he wanted again, so that he would leave and go back to the store.

When he left I went to check on Sally.

"Miss Sally," I said, as I took her lunch tray.

"Yes, Melee?" she smiled.

"I would like to help you, would you let me?" I asked.

She laughed a little, but her eyes were troubled.

"How would you help me, Melee?" she asked.

"I know some things. . .some medicine that my godmother taught me. I think that it might help you. It might heal you and make you able to, to have a child." I ducked my head down and waited, afraid that she would be angry at me for saying this. Instead she became very quiet. I waited for what seemed like forever until I dared to glance at her again.

"Yes, Melee," she whispered. "I think that I would let you help me."

After that, I went to work, trying to remember all of the recipes that Marraine had taught me and hoping that I would get it right. I knew that I needed to get a plant that did not grow near here, which only grew in the wild down in the marsh where I came from. Marraine called it Devil's Claw. I knew I could not find it for myself and I worried, wondering how I could get it. One day, an answer dawned on me.

Gabriel had come as usual to cut the grass, and as always, I brought him a mason jar of cold iced tea. He was my only visitor -- my dark angel. I looked forward to seeing his smile, so easy and free, as though nothing bad had ever touched him. We talked about his future. He wanted to go to school one day and leave this place. It was nice to dream about a future, even one I didn't share. I never thought of my own future. When I did, there was nothing there in my imagination -- only darkness.

"Miss Melee!" he beamed, as I brought him the drink. "How are you today?"

"I'm good, Gabe," I said.

I watched him as he wiped the sweat from his forehead, and then, winking at me, took the glass and downed it in one long swallow.

"Thank you kindly," he said.

"Gabe," I began, "I was wondering if you might do something for me?"

He froze for a moment and examined my face, trying to guess what I had in mind.

"Sure, anything," he answered.

"There's something that I need. A plant. Can you get it for me?"

He seemed confused for a moment, and then broke out into a laugh.

"A plant?" he grinned, "My goodness, Melee, I thought you were going to ask me for something serious!" He kept laughing and handed the glass back to me.

"Well, it is serious!" I protested, "I mean, this may not be easy to find."

"Ah. . ." he teased, "a SERIOUS plant."

I began to pout a little, wondering if I had made a mistake.

"Now, now," he soothed, "don't you fuss. I didn't say I wouldn't get it. What kind of plant do you need?" he asked, trying to erase the smile from his face.

I explained what I needed and where he might be able to find it.

"Oh, yeah," he said, thinking, "I believe I do know that plant. I think it grows down around where I take Izzy fishing with me sometimes. When do you need it?"

"Well," I answered, pushing some loose hair back behind my ears. "As soon as you can get it, but definitely before the next full moon."

"Full moon!" He exclaimed, and then burst into another laugh, "Lordy, girl, you are crazy!"

I turned deep red and stared at my feet, embarrassed. He put his finger under my chin and lifted my face up to his. I felt a shiver go down my back at his touch.

"Don't worry, now," he murmured, "if that plant's to be had in a twenty mile radius from here, I'll surely get it for you."

"Good," I sighed, "Thank you. Here, take the mason jar. You can bring it back to me in this."

Gabriel gave me another big grin and nodded, then turned back to finish his work.

True to his word, Gabe brought the Devil's Claw to me the next week. The full moon was just two nights away and I began my preparations. I had given Sally a little bit of an idea what I wanted to do. The only difficulty was getting rid of Bram for the evening. Fortunately, Sally took care of that. There was a party happening that night at the Landry's house, some kind of important social function that couldn't be missed. They both were going to go after supper, and Bram was waiting for her in the kitchen, pacing and irritated.

"Sally?" he called at the bedroom door. "Sally, we need to get going!"

She emerged wearing a bathrobe, her face ashen and her eyes barely open.

"Bram, I'm sorry. You'll have to go on without me. I just don't feel well enough to make it."

"Fine, suit yourself," he grunted, and then stomped off to the car.

As soon as he had driven away, Sally called me to her room. I brought my bag with me and began to set things up for the cleansing ceremony. I wasn't sure if I could remember everything Marraine had taught me, but I did think it would be enough. I turned off all the lights and then opened the window. The harvest moon was shining full and bright and fell in a pool on the hardwood floor. Where the moonlight shone, I sprinkled the floor with salt. I brought out the tea I had made with the Devil's Claw and placed a cup on the floor. When everything was ready, I lit a single white candle and placed it on the bedside table.

Sally was sitting on the little stool next to her dressing table, still wearing her bathrobe. As I had instructed, she had carefully bathed herself, removed all her makeup and nail polish and brushed her hair down straight and natural around her shoulders. Her eyes were large and the candle's reflection shone in her pupils. I carefully walked over and took her hands in mine and pulled her up to her feet, then I walked around behind her and pushed her gently toward the cleansing circle. As her bare feet stepped on the salt, I removed her robe from her shoulders.

Sally stood there, completely naked, bathed in moonlight. At first she dipped her head down shyly and tried to cover herself. I tugged her hands back and placed them at her side, palms up toward the moon. She closed her eyes and heaved a deep sigh. I then picked up the white candle and began slowly walking around her in clockwise circle. When I had completed the circle, I placed the candle down at her feet and the raised my cupped hands to the sky. Sally copied me.

"Moon," I said, "Come to this woman and fill her with your light. Enter her, shining in your fullness. Let your abundant power heal her and bring her all that she desires." I nodded to Sally.

"Amen," she said, and she picked up the cup of tea and took a sip. I scooped up the candle and made another circle around her, repeating my chant to the Moon. Sally continued to sip the tea, saying 'amen' each time I completed the circle. I wasn't sure if this was the right thing for her to say, but it seemed fitting. When finally she had finished the tea, I turned and slowly walked around the other direction.

"Thank you sister moon," I said. "We thank you for healing this woman. May your abundant light fill her, always."

"Amen," whispered Sally once again.

When I had completed the circle for the last time, I blew out the candle. I placed the robe back on Sally shoulders. She stood with her eyes closed for a moment in the moonlight, and then, placing her hands on her stomach, her eyes fluttered open and she smiled.

"Melee, I do believe something's different," she whispered.

"Of course it is," I smiled back. "Everything will be different now."

"Yes," she agreed, putting herself in bed, and yawning, "everything will be different now."

I stayed with her until she fell asleep and then went up to my own room.

I dreamed that night of the Vieux Diable. He was leaning over my bed, his claws reaching toward me, I could feel myself choking. I couldn't see his face, it was a shadow, a black hole, but I could hear him hissing and as his hold on my throat grew tighter and tighter, I heard him chuckling, his voice low and dreadful. I felt my lungs bursting for air, and the veins in my neck pulsing against his claws, and when the blackness began to overtake me, I woke up, gasping and screaming.

I lay shaking in my bed, afraid to move. Would he still be there when I opened my eyes? After a few minutes my breathing returned to normal and I sat up. The full moon was still shining, pouring into my bedroom window. I stood up and went to the basin to splash some cold water on my face. When I did, I peered out into the night, down into the yard, and then I saw him again! The Vieux Diable, standing just on the edge of darkness beyond the row of bushes that lined the property. I knew the dark figure was staring at the house, searching for me, but I still could not see his face.

CHAPTER THIRTEEN

Sometime during the autumn months, something strange developed between Melee and Sally. I do not know when it began, but it seemed more and more that whenever I would come home from work, I could find them together: Melee brushing Sally's hair, sitting on the back porch talking to Sally, helping Sally in the garden.

At first I was relieved. Sally had given over her hatred for the girl and learned to tolerate, then accept and finally welcome her. But as time continued, I found the relationship more and more troubling. Melee seemed to be pulling away from me, and I felt that during our time together she was only acting from obligation. She began to lie there, lifeless, as I kissed and caressed her. My passion was no longer mirrored in hers. I could feel her slipping away.

This only seemed to fuel my desire, and the more indifferent she became, the more I found myself needing her. I began to demand her every night and every day when I came home for lunch. Sometimes I would not even wait until we went up to her room, taking her in the attic, on the kitchen counter or across the dining room table. She never fought me. One time I threw her against the wall in the hallway, lifted up her skirt and took her from behind. Like an animal I rutted on her day and night, and she never complained. Yet, she became more and more like a ragdoll, limp and unfeeling. There was never any resistance from her – it was like sinking into a warm bath.

At night, when I had finished, she would stare motionless at the ceiling, humming a strange song and sometimes whispering the words in French, a song she must have known from her childhood. I would roll over next to her, exhausted, my arms wrapped tightly around her and quietly sob, hating myself for what I did, and hating her for abandoning me. Yet, no matter how tightly I clung, each morning when I awoke she was no longer there. I would find her sleeping in Sally's bed, the two of them cuddled together like sisters.

My wife and my mistress had become inseparable, and Sally would forego going out altogether, preferring to stay at home with Melee. Friends and family began asking about her. Her mother and father would visit regularly, and each time she would greet them with smiles and pleasantries, assuring them there was nothing wrong. Her father drilled me every day when I came to the store: how was Sally? Was she eating? Was she resting well? Had we seen the doctor again? And every day I reported that all was well. During the lunch rush I would go through the same routine with Boyle and Blanchard. Blanchard, of course, was especially concerned and would occasionally appear at our door in the evening to check on her. Sally was charming as ever and would greet him with a radiant smile,

"Everything's fine, Warren!" she'd say, "Never better! I am the picture of health and couldn't be happier."

"But why don't you come out, Sally?" he would ask. "We all miss you, Sugar, things just aren't the same without you there."

"Now, Warren," she'd tease, "you know as well as I do it's just the same old people at the same old gatherings doing the same old things, year after year, and I am just taking a little break."

Despite her reassurances, the good people of Techeville were not convinced, and I found myself more of an outcast than before. Sally had provided a buffer for me, and as long as she had been with me, society treated me cordially. When she was not with me, I felt the piercing eyes, heard the remark whispered behind a raised hand, and saw the disapproval on every face.

The evening of All Soul's Day, I put on a clean suit after supper and prepared to go to mass. Sally had always come with me, but that evening she locked herself in the bedroom. I knocked several times, and she did not answer, but I did hear her giggling and whispering with Melee. Irritated, I trudged off to the garage by myself, jumped in the car and headed into town to church.

The sky was darkening by the time I arrived, and the church windows glowed from within. I made my way to my regular seat, barely speaking to Sally's parents, who gave me little more than a grudging nod.

"Sally not with you again?" asked her father.

"No sir," I said, "she decided not to come."

"I just can't understand it!" fretted her mother. "I declare I think I will take her to New Orleans next month. Maybe we can do some Christmas shopping together. It might cheer her up!"

I listened for a while as Sally's parents chattered about the best way to entice Sally out of her hibernation and was grateful when the enormous blast of the organ announced that the Priest was making his way up to the altar. The mass was comforting for a change. For a while I was free from the penetrating eyes all around me, able to quietly retreat into my mind where I fretted silently about Melee.

At the end of the service, the altar boys handed out thick white candles to everyone. The candles were lit in silence, and then the Priest made his way out of the church. Row by row, the congregation followed behind, beginning with Mr. and Mrs. Landry in front, all the way through to the back of the church, and finally the colored folks who sat in the balcony.

The Priest led the long procession out of the town square and up the main road to the cemetery, about a half mile's walk. Some people joined us along the way, non-Catholics mainly who wanted to join in the evening's blessings. They lined the side of the road and fell in behind us. Among them were Annie, Izzy and Gabriel Johnson.

As the parade wound its way toward the cemetery, I reflected on how different this march was from the one I had done fifteen years ago in the heat and misery of Bataan. It seemed like a hundred years ago, so far removed was I from the fear and anguish with which I made that march. There was no angry shouting, no rifle shots, no moaning from sick and dying soldiers. Instead there was only silence except for the sound of gravel crunched underfoot, each person's bright candle creating a pool of light in the thickening darkness.

As we neared the cemetery gates, the procession slowed down, and I could hear a kind of excited murmuring from the people ahead. Something or someone was creating a stir in the congregation. The line proceeded slowly, and I saw two women standing next to the cemetery gates, one taller, holding a long white candle and the other clasped firmly to her side.

"It's Sally!" gasped her mother, who was walking directly in front of me.

Sally's parents broke out of the line and hastened to her, both embracing and kissing her. Melee was with her, and I noticed that Sally had her arm looped through the girl's. She did not let go to hug her parents, instead she pulled Melee along with her toward the procession, her mother walking at her other side. She continued to lean on Melee as she walked, like an elderly lady, seeming to need the girl's support and strength along the way.

Melee and Sally did not look at me. They fell into line with Sally's parents, just ahead of me. I assumed we were headed to the Landry family plots – the largest group of graves in the entire cemetery. This was where we went every year, following Mr. and Mrs. Landry as they walked from tombstone to tombstone, sometimes laying a candle here or there, and then waiting for the Priest to come and sprinkle holy water on each one, a benediction for the faithful departed. But Sally did not stop at the Landry graves.

"Sally?" called her mother, confused. "Where you going, honey?"

Sally did not answer, but kept on, pulling Melee along, holding her candle in front of her. Sally's parents and I followed her in silence. It suddenly dawned on me where she was going. A place she had never been, a place of which she had denied the existence for seven years. She was going to the grave of our lost child.

When she reached the lonely little headstone, she stopped, and for the first time released her grip on Melee's arm. Sally's parents and I hung back, watching her, all three of us barely able to breathe. She handed her candle over to Melee, and then knelt down in the grass in front of the stone. She lifted up her hand and cautiously, tenderly touched it and began whispering something softly, her tone gentle.

"I won't cry for you any more, dear one," she said. "I'm letting you go. You're with God now, my sweet. Wait for me. I love you."

And with that she broke into sobs, wrapping both arms around the gravestone and hugging it. Sally's mother made a movement to go to her, but her husband grabbed her by the arm and pulled her back.

"Give her a moment, Alice," he murmured. "She's needed to do this for a long time."

I wondered if I, as the father, needed to go over to her and share her grief, but my tears had long since dried out. It was really a private moment between mother and child.

When she had finished, Sally stood up and wiped her eyes, and then walked around to stand behind the gravestone. She reached for her candle from Melee and held it in one hand, keeping her other resting on the stone. She remained silent and motionless, waiting for the Priest who eventually made his way over to us, to bless the little grave. When he had finished, Sally pushed the lit candle down into the earth in front of the headstone and then slowly backed away. Her parents wrapped their arms around her, one on each side, and began to lead her out of the cemetery, Melee following closely behind.

We made our way in this fashion all the way back to town. The congregation dispersed, everyone going to their own cars and heading home. I saw Gabriel Johnson standing near our car and wondered what he could want, but before I could ask, Sally's mother spoke up.

"Darling, there's a little gathering at Grandma and Grandpa's house tonight. Would you like to go?"

Sally glanced from her mother to Melee, who nodded, and then back to her mother.

"Yes, mother, that would be nice."

"Would you like to ride with us?" asked her father, glancing at me out of the corner of his eye.

"No, no," she smiled, "I can ride with Bram." She looked back at Melee, who quickly spoke up.

"I'll be fine. Gabe said he can walk me home."

With that, Gabriel stepped out from the shadows, smiling and nodding at us all.

"Evenin' Mr. Bram, Miss Sally."

"Evening, Gabe," Sally answered. "You'll take good care of my Melee, now won't you?"

"Oh yes ma'am, yes ma'am," he assured her.

Sally turned and embraced Melee. I could sense the shock from her parents, although they said nothing.

Melee and Gabriel turned and left us, and then Sally walked over to our car. I hurried to open the door for her, and then climbed in behind the wheel. During the drive to the Landry plantation I thought of a million things to ask her, but nothing would come out. I was just too surprised to know what to say. Sally sighed and stared out her window. She wore a peaceful expression. I noticed that the bags that normally circled her eyes were missing. She seemed healthy, almost glowing. It was the first time I had really seen her in months.

When we arrived, the Grande Maison was brightly lit. Dozens of cars were parked along the driveway. I sighed, knowing that a "small gathering" at the Landry house was never less than fifty people. Sally emerged, radiant, from the car, a sparkling smile lit up her face as she climbed the steps, crossed the porch and entered the house. There were choruses of "Sally!" as aunts and uncles, nieces and nephews and cousins each embraced and kissed her, welcoming her back into the fold.

"My how we have missed you, girl!" said Old Man Landry, giving his granddaughter an extra long hug. "It's been too long."

In no time, Sally had returned to her debutante persona, laughing and flitting from conversation to conversation. I followed her around, the dutiful husband again. After an hour or so, I grew impatient, and whispered in her ear that it was getting time to leave.

I expected her to commence making her farewells, an activity which took at least twenty minutes. Instead she walked over to the buffet table, picked up a knife and began tapping it lightly on her glass. The loud buzz of the room began to die down as everyone stopped to see who was about to make an announcement. When the room was silent all eyes were turned to Sally and me.

"Well," smiled Sally, "I know that I have been making myself scarce lately and you all have been worried about me." There were a few nods and murmurs of agreement. Sally waited until the room was quiet again.

"Well there has been good reason for that. You see, I haven't been feeling myself lately." She paused, turning toward me. I shifted uncomfortably, wondering what she would say next. My pulse quickened. Would she expose me here in front of her entire family?

"The fact is that I have some very happy news to share. Bram and I," she continued, stepping closer and looping her arm through mine, "Bram and I are expecting!"

The room stayed quiet for a moment, as people stared in disbelief. I felt my mouth gape open, too shocked to speak, and then the room erupted into surprise and elation.

I stood numbly by Sally's side as each person made their way over to congratulate us. There were kisses and hugs for Sally, and several slaps on the back for me.

"Palmer, you rascal," grinned Sally's father, "I don't know how you kept this from me, but good for you!" He wrapped his arms around Sally and picked her up in an enormous hug.

"Sally darling!" shrieked Peg as she waddled over to us, tears streaming down her face, "I'm just so happy for you, I can't speak! Oh, I know things are going to go right this time, honey! And just think, now I can lend you all those clothes I've been keeping for you. Oh! I have to throw you a baby shower! When are you due?"

The two of them chattered away happily, Peg was already a week overdue, bulging like some kind of fertility goddess. She placed her hand on Sally's stomach and cooed. "Hello little one! I'll have a little cousin for you to play with whenever you're ready to come out!"

The evening wore on until almost midnight, with many more toasts, tears and congratulations. My head was spinning by the time we returned to the car. I sat gripping the steering wheel for a moment, trying to regain my composure. What the hell was Sally thinking? I was worried, really worried, that she had lost her grip on reality. I had not touched her in months. There was no way that she could be carrying a child. I churned these thoughts over and over in my head as I drove her home. How would I confront her about this? Had I, at last, driven my wife insane?

Arriving home, Sally leaped out of the car and trotted up the walkway toward the back door. Melee was waiting in the kitchen. Immediately, Sally embraced her, and the two of them started off toward the bedroom.

"Sally, wait," I called. She turned toward me, her face expectant but calm.

"Sally, I. . .I mean, are you sure? Are you sure that you're pregnant?"

"Why of course not, silly," she scoffed, shaking her head.

"I. . .I don't understand. What about your family? What you said this evening?"

"Bram," she sighed, walking toward me and placing a hand on my cheek. Her eyes were shining brightly. There was no trace of hysteria in her voice. "that was all part of the plan."

"The plan?" I blinked, astonished. "What do you mean?"

"I mean we're going to have a child, Bram, but I'm not carrying it."

Again I felt the room spinning. What was she saying? Was there something wrong with me? Was I hearing her correctly?

At that moment, Melee stepped forward and Sally wrapped her arm around her waist. Comprehension hit me like a wave. For a moment I stood staring, dumbfounded at the two of them.

"You, you mean Melee?" I stammered.

"Yes!" she exclaimed, and placed a hand over Melee's belly.

I turned from her to Melee, who nodded, confirming what I had guessed but hoped wasn't true.

"Good God, Sally, are you crazy?" I shouted, falling backwards against the kitchen table.

"Quite the contrary," she responded, her eyes narrowing and her jaw hardening with resolve. "God has seen fit to bless us with a child, Bram. At first I did not understand why Melee was brought here, and even after I did everything I could to make her go away, somehow she stayed. She was sent to us from God, Bram. She is here to bring us the child that we have always wanted."

I shook my head, beginning to panic. This was impossible. It simply could not be happening.

"We, we have to send her away," I murmured, hating myself for having to say it, but knowing it was the only way. "She has to leave, now, Sally, and we have to tell your family you've had another miscarriage." I spoke to her gently, hoping that my words would not hurt her as much as they were hurting me.

With that, Sally stepped in front of Melee, protectively.

"We will do nothing of the sort!" she hissed.

"But, Sally," I protested.

"NO!" she shouted. "No, Bram, you will NOT take this away from me! Melee WILL stay and I WILL have this child!" Her hands were shaking in fury.

I stood motionless for a moment, and then shook my head. "I can't allow that, Sally," I sighed.

"No, Bram. You WILL allow it," she growled, "Or you can go straight to hell! I will expose you for the worthless bastard you are! Everyone in this town will know what you've done to her! What you've done to me, and how long you have kept me a prisoner in my own house! I don't care if I have to live with my parents. You will get nothing from me, and you will go back to the way that I found you, a homeless nobody without two pennies to scratch together!" She spit out her words. I could see that she was determined. She was right. There was nothing I could do to stop her without losing everything.

"Sally," I whispered, "how are we going to do this? People will know. They'll see that you're not really pregnant."

"I know what I'm doing, Bram," she laughed angrily, "Melee will stay here, hidden. Her clothes will be enough to hide things until she's near the end of her term, and I can easily create an illusion. I won't be like stupid Peg Blanchard, flaunting myself in front of everyone like that. A lady shouldn't be seen in public during her final months, anyway."

I opened my mouth to speak, but then closed it. There was nothing I could say. I had to surrender.

CHAPTER FOURTEEN

The months passed, and it seemed that Sally's scheme was working. Apart from church on Sundays, she attended only the major social functions, making appearances for Thanksgiving, Christmas, and New Year's, wearing maternity clothes borrowed from Peg and complaining appropriately about her swollen feet, her aching back, nausea and fatigue. She deflected questions from Doc Collins, saying that she was seeing a specialist in Lafayette because of the extreme delicacy of her pregnancy. Peg finally gave birth to her sixth child, another baby girl, and Sally and I dutifully appeared at the Christening.

I played the role of excited father-to-be, beginning renovations to convert part of the attic into a nursery. Gifts began to arrive for the baby, wrapped in pastel colors with tiny rattles attached to the ribbons. As soon as Peg was able, she planned a shower for Sally that was held at our home. The ladies insisted on seeing the progress in the nursery and gushed over the crib, the hand-made layettes and the tiny shoes.

All the while, Melee stayed hidden. She no longer did any of the housework, and spent most of her time in Sally's bedroom or the screened-in porch. Sally took on the cooking and cleaning, and waited on Melee like a servant, rubbing her feet, massaging her shoulders and coaxing her to eat. The two were closer than ever, and Sally banished me to the spare room in the attic, bringing Melee's things to her bedroom, and sending me upstairs with mine.

I never touched Melee again after that. I hardly spoke to her, so fiercely protective had Sally become that she would often not even let me in the same room with Melee. Melee's only outside visitor was Gabriel, who would come and speak to her through the porch screen from time to time.

I had returned to my perpetual state of loneliness. My life at the store was no better, my life at home was worse. I no longer had the diversion that Melee had given me. I spent my nights alone and restless, listening to the muffled giggles and chatter of Melee and Sally below me as I curled up in the tiny bedroom in the attic. By the time Mardi Gras came, I was desperate for some kind of human companionship. I now looked forward to the festivities that I normally dreaded.

The day of the big Mardi Gras parade, the entire town shut down and the town square was decorated with gaudy streamers, balloons and banners. Vendors lined the streets selling food and drink, and bands came in from all over the parish to play music. As the day wore on, the reveling got louder and rowdier, and people began dancing in the streets, the anticipation for the big parade escalating to a frenzy.

In years past, Sally had always participated in the Mardi Gras parade, decorating a float with the Ladies Auxiliary, which they would ride in the parade, tossing beads and chocolate coins to the excited crowds. This year, of course, Sally stayed home with Melee. As I searched for a good vantage point, Warren Blanchard caught my eye and gave me a nod.

His daughter Mary-Alice saw me and squealed, "Uncle Bram! Uncle Bram!"

Though Peg and Sally were cousins, Peg had always insisted that her children call her "Auntie Sally" and thus I became Uncle Bram by default.

Mary-Alice ran to me. A tiny version of Peg, she was bubbly and frivolous, traits that were irritating coming from the mother, but quite charming in the child. The bouncy little thing grabbed my hand and dragged me toward her father who was waiting with his other children for the parade to begin.

"Come and watch with us, Uncle Bram!" She shouted. "Daddy won't let me up on his shoulders, a 'cause of his bad back, can I ride on your shoulders Uncle Bram? Can I?"

I smiled in agreement, catching the little girl under her arms and swinging her high up over my head. She erupted into shouts of glee, and sat proudly on her high perch, digging her little hands into my hair.

"Look at me, Daddy!" she crowed. "Now I can see, huh Daddy?"

"Yes, yes, now you can see you little rascal," Blanchard smiled in spite of himself, "Hey Palmer, how you doing?"

"Fine, fine," I answered, turning to crane my neck up the road to see if the parade was about to begin.

"And Sally? How is she?" he asked.

"Oh, she's fine too. Tired these days, but that's to be expected, I guess."

"Hmm," he grunted in agreement.

I was saved from further inquiries as to the health and well-being of my wife when a gun shot went off, announcing the start of the parade.

"Here it comes! Here it comes!" screamed Mary-Alice, beside herself with excitement.

There was nothing except the excited chatter of the crowd at first, and then we could hear the beating of drums and horns blowing in the distance. More than likely, the local Catholic high school band was doing the honors of leading the parade through town. The crowd grew louder and louder as the parade got closer, and Mary-Alice pulled my hair and screamed for joy. The high school band marched by in smart new uniforms, flowers festooning their hats and lapels. Then the various Krewes' floats began making their way by —

mostly silly decorated pick up trucks and trailers – with Krewe members dressed in elaborate costumes, throwing beads and chocolate candy to the crowd.

"There's Momma! There's Momma!" Mary-Alice screamed again, bouncing up and down and pointing at the float drawing near.

The Ladies Auxiliary club's float was decorated almost entirely of flowers. In years past, Sally had donated most of the roses for the float. It had been a source of pride for her, but this year she did not want to participate. In fact, her garden had been seriously neglected this year – Melee had taken up most of her time. I could see Peg Blanchard standing amongst a group of women all dressed as birds with feathery costumes and masks. Peg was hard to miss. Her costume was bright red with yellow trim and she was jumping about like a poodle, laughing, waving and throwing beads to the crowd. When she saw us, she leaned way over the side of the float and dumped a shower of beads at us.

"Catch it, baby!" she yelled, "catch it!"

Mary-Alice leaned her little hands out and grabbed at the beads falling like green, yellow and purple raindrops.

"I got one, Momma! I got one!" She was holding a fistful of shiny purple beads in triumph. Then another woman in the float dumped a load of chocolate coins on the ground, and Mary-Alice demanded to be let down so that she could join the scramble below. I pulled her off my shoulders and set her down gently in front of me. I was turning back toward the parade when I felt a heavy hand on my shoulder.

"Well, well, if it isn't Palmer!" slurred Sheriff Boyle. His breath reeked of whiskey.

"Boyle." I nodded.

"Junior, my old friend, how are you, boy?" called Boyle.

"Sheriff," Blanchard grunted. I was surprised to see that he didn't seem pleased by the sudden appearance of his old friend. In fact his face hardened and he crossed his arms across his chest.

"How's your wife, there Palmer?" asked Boyle, turning his attention back toward me.

"She's just fine, Boyle."

"Mmm hmm, yes, she sure spends a lot of time with your hired girl, uh, what's her name?" he asked, putting his arm around my shoulders. It repulsed me, and I had to force myself not to shrink away from him.

"Melee. Her name's Melee, and yes, she takes care of Sally these days."

"Yeah, Melee. . .that's right," he laughed. "Boy, she's a pretty little minx, ain't she? Man sure would have a hard time keepin' himself together with her around."

I was beginning to feel the sweat bead up on my lip. What did Boyle know? I prayed that my face did not betray the fear I was feeling. Another float went by and I took a moment to collect my thoughts.

"Course, Junior there, he wouldn't have any problems, you know, being faithful to Sally, now would you, Junior?"

Blanchard stiffened up and glared at Boyle.

"You're drunk, Sheriff. Maybe you ought to go home."

"I'll do nothin' of the sort!" shouted Boyle in mock outrage. "This here is Mardi Gras, ain't it? Folks are supposed to be havin' fun, right Palmer?" he smiled, tightening his grip around my shoulder.

"You get any leads on who stole that necklace from Meyer's?" I asked, trying to change the subject.

"Ah, yes," said Boyle, patting me on the back, "now, that's a good question. Yes, I suppose you might be interested in that." He paused for a long while, his eyes rolling up into his head. I wondered for a moment if he might fall over.

"Junior!" he yelled, suddenly, "Do we know anything about Meyer's necklace?"

Blanchard ignored him, turning his back to us and picking up Mary-Alice in his arms.

"I guess not," shrugged Boyle, "but I got a feeling I know who did it. Same ol' boy who's been lurking around town for the past six months."

"What? You mean Vernon Johnson?"

"Yes, indeed," he winked at me. Then seeing my troubled expression added, "what, didn't little Izzy tell you his long lost daddy's been comin' around?"

"Well yes, just the once, but I hadn't heard about it in awhile." Come to think of it, I had not spoken to Izzy in months, not really, anyway. So much of my thoughts had been taken up with Melee and Sally.

"Yeah, the old devil's been haunting these parts for awhile. Regular apparition he is. I never can quite seem to catch 'em at it."

"Excuse me, what did you call him?" I stammered, suddenly remembering something.

"An apparition?"

"No, no, before that, you called him an old devil, right? It reminded me of something that Melee said to me. She said she'd been seeing the devil, you know, watching her near our house. God, I thought it was just her imagination – one of those old Cajun tales. What if she was right? What if Vernon Johnson's been hiding out around our house?"

Boyle became quite serious. I could tell he was trying to shake off the whiskey fog that was clouding his thoughts.

"Hmm. Maybe so. I guess I'd better start driving by your house when I make my rounds at night. Hell, I'm already driving Annie home from Blanchard's most evenings. Guess I can swing by your place too on my way home. Pretty soon, hunting for Vernon Johnson's going to be a full-time job."

"Well I would appreciate that Sheriff, you know with Sally in the condition she's in I just don't want to take any chances."

The sheriff grunted his reply and then yelled over to Blanchard, "Hear that Junior? Palmer here wants me to start checking up on Sally for him. You don't mind now, do you?" And then to my extreme confusion, Boyle erupted into howls of laughter.

Blanchard glared over in our direction for a moment and then, setting Mary-Alice down, marched over to us. The fury in his face startled me, and I backed up a step.

"Boyle!" he seethed through gritted teeth, "like I said before, you are drunk and you need to go home."

"And like I said before, this here is a party, and I intend to enjoy myself." Boyle gathered himself up and stumbled off into the crowd.

I shook my head, amazed that the town's only real law enforcement was completely inebriated. Blanchard stood staring after him for a moment, and then turned toward me.

"Palmer, I guess it isn't a secret how I feel about you."

I blinked, unsure of where this was going.

"That being said, you are Sally's husband and the father of her unborn child, and so I do extend to you the respect and courtesy that is your due."

I waited a moment for him to continue. He seemed to be gathering his thoughts, and he closed his eyes briefly and then opened them to stare at me again.

"But I want you to know that I love Sally. I've always loved her, and I don't apologize for that. I can't love her more than as a dear sister now, I know that, but I love her just the same, and I would do anything in my power to protect her, do you understand? Anything."

I nodded, too confused to think.

"And I don't apologize for that either. Do you get me?"

"Yeah, I get you." I lied.

"Good, glad we got that straight," and with that, Blanchard turned on his heel and headed back to his children.

I could only guess at what Blanchard meant and chalked it up to yet another thinly veiled threat of what he would do to me were he to find out I had ever hurt Sally in any way. I shuddered to think of what he might do if he knew what Sally had endured over the past few months, and slowly, I began to realize myself that she had been through an ordeal.

As much as I had hated her, what I did was criminal. I was beginning to wonder if I had caused irreparable damage to Sally's mind. It could be the only explanation for the madness that was happening at my house. Never would I have ever dreamed that Sally would accept another woman's child, especially from someone whom she considered little more than dirt, and yet here she was, already maternal, wrapping a protective shield around Melee and the baby that I knew I would never penetrate. It was just too strong.

The last floats from the parade passed by and then it was at an end. The crowd dispersed, milling back into the center of the town square and getting ready for the music and dancing that would stretch on late into the night. I, on the other hand, had lost my appetite for fun. Instead I began to make my way back home. Feeling as though I needed to get some fresh air, I decided to walk.

It was a warm night for February, even for south Louisiana. The trees were already beginning to pollinate, and I saw a thin film of green covering the cars I passed along the way. The azaleas were just beginning to bloom. I felt the balmy air close around me, and it did not clear my mind. Rather it seemed to press against me, crowding my thoughts back into my head. I could not stop thinking about Sally, Melee and this strange child with two mothers. I didn't know if I could love it because it didn't truly seem to be mine. I had served my purpose in making it grow in Melee's womb and now it belonged only to her and to Sally, and I felt that my relationship with it would always be immaterial.

As I neared my house, I saw Gabriel Johnson coming out of my driveway on his bicycle. I was surprised to see him, once again. It was, after all, a holiday, and I hadn't asked him to do any projects around my house lately.

"Hey Gabe," I called to him as he pedaled up to me.

"Hey Mr. Bram, how was the parade?" He pulled his bike up and stopped, one foot on either side.

"Oh, fine," I answered. "How have you been?"

"Real good, sir, real good," he grinned at me.

"Came by to visit Melee again?"

"Yes sir, she uh, well she's my friend, sir." He shifted a bit on the seat, and stared at the ground.

"Mmm hmm," I mumbled, "Well, I expect you're the only friend she has around here."

"Yes sir," he replied, meeting my gaze, "she don't uh. . .she don't get out much."

"No, she doesn't, I suppose," I wondered if he had any idea why.

"But that's your business sir," he added.

"Well, of course you're free to visit any time," I assured him, hoping that I sounded casual enough.

"Thank you sir," was the response.

"I mean, you seem to be the only person near her age that she knows."

"Yes sir, I expect so," I could tell he was getting uncomfortable with the conversation, so I decided to change the subject.

"So, how is your mother, Gabe?"

"Fine, sir. Just fine," he said through gritted teeth, and I saw a hint of anger flash across his face.

"Your, uh, your father hasn't been coming round again, has he?"

Gabe stared at me for a moment, his eyes narrowing as if he was trying to decide something.

"No sir," he shook his head. "No, I ain't seen my father in a long time."

"You sure about that?" I questioned.

"Yes sir. Yes, I'm sure sir," he affirmed, gripping the handlebars. There was a hard edge in his voice that I couldn't quite interpret. What was he hiding?

"Well, you have a good evenin' sir," he mumbled, and without waiting for a reply he pushed off and pedaled away.

I thought about the exchange as I made my way back to the house. I had to suppose he was telling me the truth. I only hoped that if their father was back, Gabe or Izzy would feel that they could come to me. Why would they protect the man who had almost killed their mother? It didn't make sense, but then very little had made sense to me for a long time.

I let myself in through the back door, and as usual no one greeted me. Melee and Sally were locked in the bedroom as always. I rooted around in the kitchen for something to eat, and took a glass of milk and a sandwich up the stairs to the spare room that I had occupied for the past three months. Having nothing better to do, I went to bed early. I had been hoping to get a good night sleep. It had been a long time since I had really slept well, and this evening was no different. Not long after I drifted off, I began to have the most horrible nightmare I think I've ever had in my life.

I dreamt that I was lying in my bunk in the prison camp in Japan. It was nighttime, and I could hear the sounds of the men around me -- some snoring, some moaning in pain and some muttering nonsense, their frightened tones letting me know they were having a nightmare.

I got up to go to the latrine, and as I stepped into the black night, I was struck by how quiet it was out in the camp. The prison guards who normally patrolled were missing. I suddenly got the strange feeling that we were alone, and that there were no guards around, although I could not imagine where they had gone. I paused for a moment, listening to the silence and staring out into the darkness, wondering if now was my chance to escape.

Everything in me screamed that I should not do it. At any moment, I knew a guard could see me and shoot me in the back, or worse, shoot me in the leg, drag me back, and then flog me senseless the next day in front of the entire camp. When I was gasping for mercy, he would run a bayonet through me or cut off my head.

Despite this knowledge and the paralyzing fear it generated, I felt compelled to go, and so before I could stop myself I was hunched over, running from the latrine to the barracks and further out to the edge of the camp. I tried to keep my body in the shadows as much as possible, but there was a full moon out and the camp was flooded with an eerie light. I could hear my heart pounding in my ears and fought to control the panic welling up in my chest.

I made it to the fence, a flimsy wooden thing that served little more than to mark the borders of the camp. The next moment I was scaling it. When I reached the top, I took one last look behind to see if I had raised the alarm, and then I saw it – a dark figure moving slowly toward me.

It was not a guard. It did not move like a soldier. It was tall, inhumanly tall, and covered an impossible amount of ground with each stride it took. It glided along as if it did not need to hurry, as if my capture was inevitable. The moon was shining behind it, casting what would have been a face in complete shadow. It had no weapon, but I knew that its purpose was to kill me.

In terror, I flipped myself over the top of the fence and came down hard. I heard the bone in my right ankle snap and felt white hot flames of pain shooting up my leg. Now I was hobbling along, dragging my foot beside me. Just beyond the fence was a ditch, built from the sweat of the soldiers living in the camp. It was used for water run-off from the torrential rains that sometimes swept through. The ground was muddy and slick. I slid down the first side, a shock of pain washing through me as my foot stopped my fall. Nausea overcame me and I rolled over in the mud and vomited. When I rolled back over, I saw my demonic pursuer sailing over the top of the fence behind.

I knew that it would reach me in just a few more strides, and I struggled to my feet. I began to sob uncontrollably, the tears pouring down my cheeks and my breath coming in ragged pants as I fought my way through the mud that sucked me downward with every step. I reached the other side of the ditch and looked back. The black figure was standing at the top of the ditch now. It paused for a moment and stared at me, and then slowly raised its arm to point at me. I felt myself screaming, trying furiously to scramble up the other side. My frenzied scrambling did nothing but pull huge clumps of mud down the sides and into the ditch. I could not climb it.

I knew that my killer was right behind me now, and I shrank into the side of the ditch, pressing my back into it and covering my eyes with my hands. I waited for death, but the thing did not strike. I could feel it towering above me and for one instant took my hands from my face and looked up. It was bending over me, its arms extended toward my neck and I knew it meant to strangle me. I braced for the feel of its cold fingers encircling my neck and squeezed my eyes closed again, knowing that this was the end and praying for it to come quickly. The next moment my mind went black and everything faded into nothing.

CHAPTER FIFTEEN

I woke up gasping and clutching my throat. My cry echoed around the tiny room for a moment, and then all was silent. I eyed the clock next to the bed and saw that it was after midnight. My clothes and sheets were soaked in sweat, so I sat up in the bed for a moment. It had been years since I'd had a dream like that. After the war, I had them nearly every night that I wasn't drinking. Most of the time I'd try to drink as much as possible during the day so that I'd pass out. The liquor would drown out my dreams, and sleep became a black nothingness, a period of unconsciousness to break up the nightmare of my waking hours. After I married Sally, the dreams came less frequently, and she would be there to calm me in the night, until finally they subsided altogether. I suppose I was naïve to think that they would never come again.

I knew that I would not be able to fall back asleep, and so I got out of bed to try and bring myself back into the present. The moon was shining brightly into the room, and I walked over to the washing stand to splash some cold water on my face. I grabbed the towel and held it over my eyes, beginning to breathe normally again. When I pulled the towel away and glanced down out the window, I saw something that made me freeze. It was a figure standing just beyond the driveway under the cover of a row of azalea bushes. Just like the figure in my dream, I could not see its face. I knew immediately that this must be Melee's devil, and yet this was no demon. It was clearly a man.

My fear quickly turned to anger, and the next instant I was running across the attic, barreling down the steps, fumbling with the kitchen door and then leaping down the back steps and out into the night. I ran around to the side of the house where I had seen the stranger, but he was gone. I stopped in my tracks, listening intently, trying to determine if I could hear him. There was nothing but a strange silence. The usual chirp of crickets and call of night birds was noticeably absent. I felt a suppressive feeling of dread in the air as though the stranger had left a wake of malice behind him.

I ran down the driveway and out into the road and stood there turning back and forth, searching up one way and down the other, straining my eyes in the hope that I would see some kind of movement in the shadows.

"Who are you?!" I shouted.

I waited for a reply but heard nothing.

"What do you want?!" I shouted again.

A dog started barking in the distance.

I stood thinking about my options, wondering if I should get in my car and hunt for him, and then thought better of it. Whoever it was, he was gone and hopefully would not be back.

I went back to the house and after letting myself inside, locked the back door and then walked to the front door to make sure it was locked too. All was silent. If Melee and Sally had heard the commotion of my running out into the street and yelling for the stranger, there was no sign of it. I was grateful for that. It meant that I could spend the rest of the night alone.

I turned off the kitchen lights, poured myself a brandy and proceeded to sit in the dark in a large leather arm chair, smoking and slowly sipping my drink. Tomorrow was Ash Wednesday, I thought, flicking my cigarette into the ashtray. Peg Blanchard would be giving up chocolate as she did every year. Her husband would abstain from alcohol and complain about it at every opportunity. I would not need to do anything more than I already did. For years my life had been one long Lenten season of abstinence and deprivation. The time with Melee was a momentary lapse in my solitary and celibate existence. Now that it was over, I was even more acutely aware of my loneliness, and I felt it like a pang of hunger in the pit of my stomach.

At some point during the night I must have dozed off again, because I woke up to the sound of a blue jay screeching outside my window. I was thankful to have made it through the night without another nightmare. From the brightness of the sun I could tell that it was already quite late in the morning. I dragged myself out of the chair, and was struck by a searing headache so I shuffled into the kitchen to find some coffee.

Melee was seated at the table, peeling potatoes into a large ceramic bowl. When I walked in she jumped as though I had scared her. It was the first time I had seen her without Sally in months. She stared at me, open mouthed, fear washing over her face.

"Good morning," I said, "sorry if I frightened you." I walked around the table and opened up the kitchen cabinet to grab a mug.

"I- I thought you were at work," she stammered.

I scanned the clock on the wall. It was nearly ten in the morning. Months ago, I would have panicked, knowing that my father-in-law would be waiting for me at the store, ready to launch into a tirade about my shiftlessness, my irresponsibility and general failure as a man. Now I didn't care. Charlie Bordelon and his wife Alice were excitedly waiting for the birth of Sally's imaginary child. Their elation at the prospect of becoming grandparents had erased most of their animosity toward me. I enjoyed taking advantage of their short-lived goodwill.

I poured myself some coffee and drank it down. It was probably made some time in the early hours and was now quite cold, but its bitterness helped to wake me up and clear my mind. I noticed that Melee had not recommenced her task at the table. Instead she was watching me closely. Over the last few months she had become terrified of me. It was sickening to think that I now repulsed her, although I had only myself to blame. My blinding need for her had driven me to do things that I now regretted. It was true that I had used her. I had taken advantage of her vulnerability and forced myself on her time and again, deluding myself into thinking that she was willing. It was only Sally's intervention that had stopped me.

Even now as I stared at her I could feel the desire begin to prick at me. Her flushed cheeks and pregnant belly made her seem all the more beautiful and mysterious to me. I wondered how it would feel to hold her again, and feel her warmth against my chest. I imagined her enlarged breasts swaying gently as she moved up and down on me, her eyes closed and her head leaned back in pleasure. My momentary reverie was broken by the loud bang of the screen door announcing Sally's entrance into the kitchen.

My wife stood motionless, taking in the scene. Her eyes flitted from my face to Melee's and back to mine. She gritted her teeth and glared at me.

"What are you doing here?" she snapped, removing her gloves and hat and setting them down on the kitchen counter. She was wearing a ridiculous maternity dress, and I could see she had concocted some kind of padding underneath. The effect was convincing, although she did not have the natural color and softness in her face that Melee's possessed.

"I had some dreams last night," I answered, dumping the rest of my coffee in the sink and rinsing out my mug. "I came downstairs and fell asleep in a chair, and I guess I overslept."

I noticed a smudge of ash on Sally's forehead. Presumably she had gone to mass this morning, perhaps with her mother or Peg Blanchard. She walked over to Melee and stood behind her, her hands resting protectively on the girl's shoulders. Melee raised up her right hand and placed it over Sally's.

"I guess you'd better get going then," grumbled Sally, "Daddy will be expecting you at the store." She patted Melee's shoulder, and then helped her up out of the chair. The two of them went back to the bedroom together without another word.

I did my best to pull myself together. After a quick wash and shave, I dressed myself in a hopelessly wrinkled shirt and pair of pants. Neither Melee nor Sally bothered with the ironing anymore at least not any of my clothes, and I had to admit I looked terrible. When I arrived at the store that morning, it was eleven o'clock and time to set up for the lunch counter.

"Well, welcome, Palmer," Bordelon called across the store, his voice brimming with sarcasm. "Glad you could make it. Boy, you look rough. Have too much fun at the parade yesterday?"

"Oh, not too much, sir," I shrugged, "Guess I didn't get too much sleep last night, Sally was up quite a bit," I lied.

Bordelon's face immediately turned serious and he walked over to me. "Everything alright?" he asked, "She's not feeling poorly is she? Alice took her to mass this morning, but she didn't mention anything."

"Oh no, she's fine," I smiled, "Just the usual discomfort."

"I see, I see," Bordelon nodded, the subject was distasteful to him and he quickly changed the subject. "Alright then, Bram. I'll let you get over to the lunch counter." He strode off to the front of the store where a customer was waiting.

I took my time setting up for lunch. My head was still pounding and I was beginning to feel a bit nauseated from lack of food. I was putting coffee cups and saucers on the counter when Warren Blanchard walked up and seated himself on his usual stool.

"Hey Palmer," he nodded, flipping over his coffee cup.

I poured him a cup and then stepped back for a moment.

"Where's the Sherriff?" I asked him, noticing the conspicuous absence of his usual crony.

"Hell if I know," he grumbled, "lying in a hole somewhere would be my guess. Damn fool got drunk as a skunk last night."

I was surprised at Blanchard's anger. I had never seen him speak in that manner about Boyle. As far as I knew, they were partners if not friends. Blanchard noticed my confusion.

"He ain't been acting right for months," Blanchard muttered in a low voice. "I don't know what's wrong with him, but he's downright embarrassing. Not showing up in court, coming to my office with liquor on his breath, I'm telling you I'm gonna have to cut him loose," he shifted on his stool, twisting his head around to see if anyone was listening. "Palmer, that idiot has become a liability to me. I have a reputation to maintain, and I'll be damned if I'm gonna have it tarnished by a sleazy miscreant like that."

"Miscreant!' I exclaimed, "Jesus, Junior, what's Boyle done?"

Blanchard sat up straight and glared at me, suddenly realizing he had said too much.

"Don't worry about it, Palmer," he said, "I'm taking care of it."

He would say no more. I was disturbed by the revelation. I had hoped to talk to Boyle about the stranger I'd seen last night outside the window. Now I wondered if it was worth it. Boyle's days as Sherriff would be numbered as soon as Blanchard decided he was no longer fit for the job.

After the lunch rush was over, I cleaned up and went to the stockroom to do some inventory. My thoughts were interrupted by a light tap at the door. It was Izzy Johnson.

"Hi Mr. Bram," he mumbled. "You got any deliveries for me today?"

His head was turned away from me, a baseball cap clutched tightly in his hands.

"Yeah, I think we do, Izzy," I answered. "I'll just get the order list."

I walked toward him and noticed that he was keeping his head down, his normal smile absent.

"Izzy," I said, "what's wrong, son?"

He looked up at me, and I gasped. The left side of his face was bruised and swollen. Tears were welling up in his eyes.

"N-nothing, sir," he said, quickly brushing away the moisture on his cheek.

I pulled him into the stockroom and shut the door.

"Izzy," I said, "don't tell me nothing's wrong. Who hit you?"

"Nobody sir," he said, "I- I was playin' ball with Gabriel and uh, I missed. He threw a hard one to me and it hit me in the face. It was just an accident, sir."

"Izzy, that doesn't look like a ball hit you." I shook my head and put my hands on his shoulders. "You can tell me, you know. I want to help you."

Izzy stood staring at me for a moment, his mouth opening as if he were about to say something. Then he turned his head away again.

"No sir," he said. "It was an accident."

"Izzy, I know your father has been around again. I know that he's been hitting your mother and now he's hit you, hasn't he son?"

"No sir," Izzy mumbled.

"Yes he has, son. Why are you protecting him? You don't need to be afraid, Izzy. I can help you. Let me help you, Izzy."

Izzy was crying in earnest now.

"I got to go, Mr. Bram," he cried. "I – I need to go home. I forgot my momma wanted me to do something for her."

He moved toward the door and started to open it.

"No Izzy," I pleaded, "don't go. Let me drive you home at least. Maybe I can talk to your momma. Is she home today?"

"No sir, she's at Mrs. Peg's house," said Izzy. "I got to go, sir, please, sir."

He was getting panicky now, his voice trembling. He turned the door knob and pushed the door open.

"Alright, alright," I tried to calm him, "it's ok, Izzy. You can go."

With that, Izzy jammed his cap back on his head and bounded out of the back of the store. I went after him and watched as he climbed on his bike and pedaled away.

It was the last time I would see him for weeks. Every day I would wait for him, hoping that the sunny little boy would come skipping back into the store, but he did not return. I began to do the deliveries myself, and took to driving down to the Bottoms from time to time, cruising up one street and down another to see if I could spot Izzy's bicycle parked somewhere. I drove slowly, dodging potholes and mangy stray dogs along the muddy gravel road. The tiny shotgun houses drifted by, one looking very much like another, the same plastic chairs and wooden benches adorning the porches and the same tired old colored women sitting in rocking chairs, snapping beans and raising their heads in surprise to see me and my shiny car. I would wave and they would lift a tentative hand in reply, wondering what a white man was doing so far away from town.

I wanted to question Gabriel, but he too was missing for weeks. I determined that he did come to the house, as I would find the yard cut, the hedges trimmed and various other odd jobs completed but never did I see him. It seemed that he timed his visits to coincide with my absence. One Saturday, however, I came home early and found him sweeping the driveway. I parked my car in the garage and then walked over to him, determined to get a real answer to my questions this time.

"Hello Gabe," I called, "how you been?"

"Fine, sir, fine," he smiled, pausing to wipe the sweat off his face.

"And your mother?"

"She fine too, sir," he smiled again.

"You know, Gabriel, I haven't seen your brother around lately. In fact it's been weeks. It's not like him to not come to the store."

Gabriel nodded and scratched the back of his neck.

"Yeah, I'm sorry about that. I guess Izzy didn't come to tell you goodbye."

"Goodbye?" I asked, surprised. "Where did he go?"

"Oh, he's with my Aunt Betty in Baton Rouge, sir. Yeah, he went out to visit, you know. I got a whole heap of cousins up there and Izzy loves to go and play with 'em."

I stared at Gabriel for a moment. There was something about the way he spoke that wasn't convincing.

"Are you sure about that?" I asked.

"Sure about what, sir? That Izzy went to my aunt's house? Yes sir, I'm sure about that," he chuckled and cracked another smile.

"No, I mean are you sure that's why Izzy went to your aunt's house? Just to visit? There wouldn't be any other reason?"

The smile left Gabriel's face and he began to shift uncomfortably.

"I'm not sure what you mean, sir. What other reason would there be?"

I took a deep breath, and then unleashed the frustration I'd been feeling for weeks.

"Come on, Gabriel, I know what's been going on. The sheriff told me."

Gabriel's jaw clenched and a flicker of anger darkened his expression.

"Oh, yeah, what did the sheriff say?" he demanded.

"That your daddy's back. That he's been wandering around town. That he's been beating on your mother, and I'm guessing your brother too. That's why he was sent away, isn't it? To keep him away from your father?"

Gabriel started at me for a moment, and then broke into an angry laugh.

I ignored it, and continued on.

"Let me help you, Gabe. I think you and Izzy have a future. I really think you could make something of yourselves if you tried."

I don't know what compelled me to want to do something for Izzy and Gabe. Surely my wife, her parents and most of Techeville would think I was crazy, but I simply felt that after all the harm I'd done in the world, perhaps this was my chance to do some good.

Gabriel closed his eyes and shook his head.

"Help us, Mr. Bram? What do you think a white man could do to help a colored boy like me?"

I winced at his words and opened my mouth to speak, but he cut me off.

"You think you gonna call the sheriff? Think he's gonna care about my momma and my no-good father?"

His voice was angry. I had never seen Gabriel angry.

"Or, maybe you think you gonna call Mr. Blanchard? Think he'd come down to the Bottoms, dressed in his fine fine suit and bring my daddy to justice? No, Mr. Bram, I expect there ain't nothin' under the sun that a white man could do to help me, and I don't believe I'd let him if he could."

With that, he picked up the broom and tipped his hat to me.

"I best be going, Mr. Bram. I thank you for your offer, but this really ain't no concern of yours."

Gabe strode back toward the garage to put away the broom and the lawnmower and collect his bicycle. He was gone a few minutes later, and I was left with the gnawing feeling that he had left something unsaid and that I might never know what that could be.

CHAPTER SIXTEEN

Hail Mary, full of grace, the Lord is with thee. Blessed art thou among women and blessed is the fruit of thy womb. Holy Mary, Mother of God, pray for us sinners, now and at the hour of our death.

And so I pray to the blessed Virgin every day, the words that the angel Gabriel spoke to her when she, like I, was a young woman, unmarried and carrying a child. I wonder if she had known what I know: the joy of feeling the life growing inside her and the fear that she would be an outcast, condemned to live a life of shame, and her child branded a bastard.

I felt these things the moment that I knew. It started soon after the moon blessing that I had performed with Sally. I woke up one morning and vomited in the sink as I made breakfast, the smell of bacon made me sick. Then I became so tired and wanted only to sleep, and I could not understand it. Never had I felt so weary, and I would find myself dozing off on my feet as I hung the laundry up to dry.

The realization of what was happening to me hit me hard, and I became very afraid. Where would I go? I could never go back to my father. Marraine and my grandmother were long since dead. Would Sally cast me out? Would I be sent away to wander the streets of New Orleans, forced to become the whore that my father always told me I'd be? I was little more than a whore now. I had allowed Mr. Bram to take me because I wanted to stay, and the consequence was that now I would have to leave.

I became more and more panicked about it, knowing that soon I would not be able to hide the truth. One morning after Bram left for the store, I went outside to cut flowers for Sally. The day was hot, and I began to sweat as I clipped blooms from the rose bushes the way that Sally had taught me. I was reaching up, high above my head to clip a beautiful pale pink blossom, when the sun blinded my eyes. I felt my heart pounding and heard the blood rushing in my head and then I blacked out.

I had the sensation that I was sinking into the earth, and I felt the warm dirt pressed against my cheek. Then I felt warm hands around me, grabbing me beneath the arms and pulling me up. I was lifted into someone's arms and carried into the house.

"Miss Sally, come quick!" I heard a familiar voice calling.

It was Gabriel. He smelled like fresh cut grass, and I leaned my head against his chest and let myself relax into him. He had always been a comfort to me, my only comfort in this isolated world I lived in. He was the only one who did not want anything from me, except to be my friend.

Gabriel put me down on a chair in the kitchen and leaned me against the table. I opened my eyes and began to be able to see again. I felt Sally standing behind me, her cool hands against my back, supporting me. Gabriel ran to the sink and grabbed a glass of water and brought it back to me.

"Gabriel, quick, get that towel there wet and bring it to me."

Moments later I felt the cool towel pressed against the back of my neck. The darkness was leaving me, and I looked up to see Gabriel holding the glass in front of me, an expression of worry and compassion on his face.

"Melee, can you hear me?" Sally whispered, stroking my back.

She was so nice to me now. So different from how she was before. She was my friend, like Mathilde had been, but I knew that it would be over soon. Her friendship was only a brief respite for me, a protective embrace that I had felt from Marraine and my grandmother and even spoiled Mathilde for a short time. Her love would be taken away from me just as my mother's had been, and I would once again be alone. The thought of this overcame me, and I burst into tears.

"Shh, shh," soothed Sally, "you're alright now, Sugar, everything's alright. You just got yourself overheated, that's all. My goodness your face is red! Gabriel, take her to my room and lay her down on the bed."

Gabriel lifted me up again, and carried me to the bedroom. I sank down into the cool quilt and closed my eyes. Sally put the wet towel over my eyes and stroked my arm softly.

"Miss Sally, you want me to go get Doc Collins?" Gabriel asked.

"NO!" I shouted, sitting up in bed. The last thing I wanted was an examination. I knew that my secret would be revealed, but that was not the way I wanted it to happen.

"It's alright, Melee, honey, don't worry. We don't have to call him right now," said Sally. "Thank you, Gabriel. I think we'll be alright, but stay close to the house in case I need you."

"Yes ma'am," Gabe answered. "I'll be right out the back door, you hear, Melee?"

I nodded and then closed my eyes again.

Sally pulled a chair over to the bedside and sat next to me for a long time, not speaking but humming a tune softly. I wanted so much to just rest. To fall asleep and wake up somewhere that I could be safe forever and never be afraid again, but I knew that this was a false hope. There was no haven for me. There was nowhere that I could go. Again, the desperation overwhelmed me, and I began to sob.

"Hush now, honey," Sally crooned, pulling me up and putting her arms around me. "What's wrong with you? You can tell me."

"Oh, Miss Sally, I wish that I could, but I can't!" I choked the words out between my sobs.

"Melee, there isn't anything you could tell me that I wouldn't be able to hear." Sally pulled my face up to look into her eyes, and I saw nothing but honesty and sympathy there.

"Please, Sally," I begged, "don't send me away, please." I whispered.

"Never, Melee," she promised, "I'll never send you away. I don't care what it is."

I sat silently for a while, tears spilling out over my cheeks, my hands gripping the quilt. I knew that once I told her she would push me away in anger. Most likely she would send me to pack my things and then she would turn me out of the house and lock the door.

"Melee," Sally murmured. "I know what my husband has done to you."

I nodded. Sally had endured Mr. Bram's obsession as much as I had.

"Melee," she said again, "It isn't your fault."

I looked up at her and saw understanding in her eyes.

"But Miss Sally, what am I going to do?" I cried. Sally moved over to sit beside me on the bed and pulled my head against my chest.

"Melee, you are going to stay here, and I am going to take care of you," she said. "I understand now why you were sent here. You were the answer to my prayers. You are a gift from God, Melee. I didn't understand it before, but now I do."

I was shaking. Was it possible that Sally already knew the truth and was telling me that she was not angry about it? I looked up at her face again, and she smiled at me.

"Dry those tears, honey, don't you worry about a thing. This is not a time to be sad. This is a time to celebrate. I asked God for a child, but I couldn't have one myself, so He sent you to me. This is our child, Melee, yours and mine. I will raise it as my own, and you will stay here to help me. You never have to worry about anything again."

Once again, I was confused. What exactly was she saying?

"But, Miss Sally," I whispered, "everyone will know it's my child. No one will accept it."

"Nonsense!" she exclaimed, and I saw an expression of rapture on her face. "No one will know, Melee, I'll make sure of that. They will think it is mine, and I will raise it myself. No harm or shame will come to you, I promise."

A chill went down my back as I realized what Sally was saying. She was going to take my baby from me. I would have it, but it would never be mine. She saw the confusion on my face and spoke again.

"Melee, you can't possibly raise this child on your own. Where would you go? How would you feed it? Think of everything I could give it! A good home, a good education, everything that money can buy, and you, my darling, will be a part of it. You'll be giving it all this too!"

I nodded. She was right. If I left, most likely the child would be dead before its first birthday, and I would not live much longer after it. If I stayed I could watch it grow up, seeing it have everything in life that I would never be able to give it. There wasn't a real choice to be made. It was the only way.

"Alright, Miss Sally," I agreed.

Sally gave a cry for joy and hugged me to her tightly. Things began to change immediately. She moved all my belongings to her bedroom and instructed me that I was never to sleep upstairs nor have any contact with Bram again. There was no argument from me. I was so relieved to no longer be the object of his obsession. Instead I became Sally's. She protected me like a tiger. I was given everything I could ever want or need. She fed me, clothed me, and cared for me better than my own mother could have. Every day, she would press her ear against my belly and whisper to the baby. She was overjoyed to feel the baby kick. She would wrap her arms around me and hold my belly every night in her sleep.

Her masquerade to the outside world was perfect. Everyone, except Bram, thought that she was truly pregnant. It was only home alone that she would take off the disguise, but I saw that it made her feel even more a part of my pregnancy. By acting as if she were carrying the child, she began to believe that she actually was. Gradually, her adoration of me began to cool. I became little more than the vessel that carried precious cargo. She remained caring and protective, but it was not for me, it was only for the baby, and I began to fear that once I had it, she would no longer need me.

Her charade also depended on my being completely hidden from view, and so I spent the long months wandering the rooms of the house, and occasionally sitting outside in the screened porch. When Bram was home, Sally locked me in her room. She even brought in a chamber pot so that I would not need to cross the hallway to the bathroom. I was not allowed out of the house anymore. I longed to feel the wind on my face and the grass under my feet, but I was kept a prisoner – pampered, coddled and fussed over – but a prisoner nonetheless.

Finally it became too much to bear and one afternoon when Sally had gone out and Bram was at the store, I went and sat in the screened-in porch and cried.

"Melee, is that you?" a voice interrupted me.

I sat up and peeked out the screen. It was Gabriel. I sighed in relief, and then stood up to walk over to the side of the porch where he was standing. I knew that he would be able to see me, even through the black screen, but I didn't care. I wanted so much to hear another human voice. It had been so long since anyone besides Sally had spoken to me.

"Gabe!" I smiled, "how you been?"

"Good girl! How bout yourself?" he smiled.

"Oh, I'm fine," I answered, but my voice betrayed me and I had to stifle back my tears.

"Melee," he murmured in a low voice. "I miss you. I know you're not happy there. Let me take you somewhere."

I began to really cry now. I missed him terribly, my only friend, and yet I knew that I would never be allowed to go anywhere near him.

"Melee, honey, don't cry," he whispered, and put his hand up against the screen. I put my hand up too, and could feel the warmth of his hand through the wire mesh.

"How, Gabe?" I asked, "how you gone get me out of here?"

"Don't you worry about that!" he beamed. "When will Miss Sally and Mr. Bram be away?" he asked.

"Well," I thought for a moment, "next week is Palm Sunday. I guess they will go to church and then to the Landry house for the afternoon. They most likely won't be home until suppertime."

"There you go!" he crowed, "that's it! I'll come and get you next week, then. My cousin has a truck. We'll come over here in the morning, after Miss Sally and Mr. Bram leave, and you'll come with me, alright?"

I began to think that the plan might work. "Go where, Gabe?" I asked. "And how will you get me out of here? Miss Sally locks me in the room."

"Locks you in the. . ." he started, then shook his head, "never mind that, Melee. Just you never mind. I fix enough broken doors to know how to jimmy one open. You just be ready next Sunday for me, you hear?"

I nodded, suddenly feeling hopeful. Perhaps this would work, after all.

The days leading up to Palm Sunday dragged by slower than any week in the previous six months. I became more and more anxious as time wore on. When the day finally arrived I was nearly ready to burst. I worked hard to contain my excitement and waited until Sally finally got herself ready to go.

"I'll be back this evening, alright?" she said. "Bram won't be home, so

I'll leave the door unlocked and you can go to the kitchen if you need to. I made you some sandwiches and put them in the icebox for you, okay?"

"Yes, thank you," I smiled.

"Be sure you eat, now, you hear?" she fussed. I needed to remember to take those sandwiches with me. Sally would be angry if she came home and thought that I had starved myself.

"Yes, I will," I agreed.

After more fussing and admonishing to stay off my feet and rest, she finally left with Bram. It was one of the few times that she had done so in months. Sally associated with Bram as little as possible, and usually only for obligatory functions. Palm Sunday was one of them. Sally had told me that her family held a large gathering every year at the Landry plantation. Of course, they did so for every major holiday and celebration, and I wondered that they would not be doing exactly the same thing next week for Easter.

I did not have to wait too long for Gabriel to arrive. It seemed only a few minutes after the rumble of Bram's car disappeared down the road, I heard the loud banging of an ancient engine approaching. I ran out to the kitchen to wait at the back door. A hopelessly beat up old truck appeared around the corner. One of its fenders was missing, and the body was covered in rust, with most of the paint peeling off. I was horrified for a moment that it reminded me of my father's old truck, but shook off the feelings of revulsion. This was not my father coming back to get and drag me away. This was Gabriel, come to rescue me.

The truck came to a stop behind the house and Gabriel bound out the passenger door, a huge grin plastered on his face. I left the house and made my way down the stairs, and he caught me up into a bear hug. I worried for a moment that he would feel my belly. I was sure that he had, but he did not seem to notice or mind it if he did. I had worn an old dress that Peg had given Sally. Not too fancy, but nice. It was very large, and swallowed me up, and I hoped that people would think that I was just a poor girl who had no clothes and had to wear dreadful hand-me-downs.

"You ready to go have some fun?" asked Gabriel, doing a little dance from side to side.

"You know it!" I grinned in return.

The next instant, Gabriel was lifting me up off my feet. I grabbed his neck and gasped in surprise. He lifted me up over the side of the truck and put me into the back. There I saw a large quilt spread out. Gabriel leaped in after me, and then gave me a sheepish grin.

"Sorry about this," he explained. "I know you don't wanna be seen, so I expect you'll need to lie down here in the back. There ain't enough room for you in the cab to get down on the floor." I nodded in agreement.

"Hope you don't mind it too much," he added. "I'll stay back here with you, if that's alright."

"Sure, that's alright," I murmured.

Gabriel lay across the quilt and pulled me down next to him. He put his arm around me and I leaned my head against his shoulder. Then he pounded a fist against the back of the cab to let his cousin know we were ready to leave.

It was a giddy, bouncy ride from the Palmer's house down to the Bottoms. Gabe's cousin took it as slow as he could, so not to jar us too much. I gazed straight up and saw blue sky, sometimes broken up by tree branches or a bird passing overhead. When we drove through town, I heard the sound of the church bell ringing and knew that Sally and Bram would be going in for mass holding palm leaves, the priest leading them in the annual procession. Occasionally the truck would hit a hard bump or pothole and Gabriel would fly up into the air for a moment. Each time he would ask me if I was alright and each time I would giggle in reply.

When we finally arrived at his house, it was getting late in the morning.

The truck stopped and Gabriel sat up and checked around.

"Coast is clear," he winked at me, and then pulled me up on my feet.

We were parked in front of a tiny wood framed house. It was painted a bright robin's egg blue and had white columns holding up a front porch. Seated in a rocking chair was an old woman. She smiled up at us and waved.

"Grandma!" shouted Gabriel, bounding towards the woman. He bent over and hugged her and then she grinned a toothless smile and patted his cheek.

"Grandma, there's someone I'd like for you to meet," he gestured toward me. I walked to him, shyly, wondering what his grandmother would think of me. She held out two wrinkled and gnarled hands toward me, and I placed my hands in hers.

"Grandma, this is Melee," said Gabriel.

She peered at me through narrowed eyes. I could see the cataracts in them and knew that she must be nearly blind.

"Hello, child," she whispered. "Lay your troubles at the door, Sugar, you safe enough here," and she gave my hand a squeeze and then released me. Gabriel grabbed my hand and pulled me toward the door. Izzy was standing there, hopping from one foot to the other.

"Miss Melee!" he shouted, overjoyed. I smiled and gave him a hug.

"Izzy I ain't seen you in so long, where you been?" I asked. He was about to answer when a woman's voice called from the other room.

"ISRAEL JOHNSON! You get back in this kitchen this instant! I done told you I need you to take out this trash!"

"OK MOMMA!" Izzy hollered back. He rolled his eyes, and then gave a me a wink and ran off toward the back of the house.

Gabriel ushered me inside where I was greeted by heavenly smells: baked ham, fried chicken, mashed potatoes and gravy, collared greens, black-eyed peas and homemade biscuits. I recognized each distinct smell. It reminded me of Marraine's house so many years ago.

"Momma she's here, she's here, she's here!" I could hear Izzy shouting excitedly.

"Hush child, yes, I know, now get this trash on out of here!"

The next moment, Gabe's mother emerged from the kitchen, wiping her hands on her apron. Annie Johnson was a beautiful woman. Her black hair was pulled back in a bun, and wisps of it floated around her head like a halo. She was sweating a little, giving her dark skin a polished glow. She was petite and her features were small and delicate, but her arms were quite muscular and she seemed incredibly strong. She held her arms out and took my hand in hers, staring directly into my eyes.

"Miss Melee, my son has told me so much about you. It's a pleasure to meet you."

I blushed, unused to such genuine kindness.

"Thank you, ma'am," I replied, "thank you for having me."

"I hope you're hungry!" she smiled.

Gabriel slipped his arm around me and led me to the kitchen. The room was hot and the windows were steamy from all of the cooking that Annie must have been doing since early in the morning. I realized that Gabe's family was going out of their way for me. I was sure that they must have skipped church that morning, and I felt a pang of guilt when I realized that Annie, who worked so hard every day of the week, was spending her only day off cooking for me. We kept going through the back door, where a picnic table was waiting under a live oak tree, a blue checked table cloth covering it. The dishes and silverware were already set. Gabriel led me to the table and helped me get seated.

"I'll be right back!" he promised.

For the next few minutes, Gabe, Izzy and Annie scurried back and forth between the kitchen and the picnic table, bringing food bowls, bread baskets, lemonade and iced tea. When all was nearly ready, Gabe went around the front of the house and returned a few minutes later, pushing his grandmother in a rickety old wheel chair.

When everyone was seated, Annie took Gabe and Izzy's hands, seated one on either side of her and bowed her head. Gabe grabbed my hand, and his grandmother took the other. We all bowed our heads and waited for Annie.

"Dear God, we thank you today for family and for the joy that family brings."

"Yes, Lord," whispered Gabe's grandma.

"God, we just lift up those seated here at this table, that you might wrap your loving arms around them, Lord."

"Praise you Jesus!" the old woman mumbled.

"And God, I want to thank you for our guest, Miss Melee, bless her, dear Lord, protect her and bring her not into temptation but deliver her from evil."

"Praise God!" Gabe's grandmother was getting louder.

"And God we just ask all these things in your son's precious name, Amen."

All around the table echoed Annie's "amen" and then Izzy's hand darted toward the basket of biscuits. Without looking up, Annie reached over and slapped it.

"Mind your manners, boy!" she snapped. "We are going to serve our guests, first."

Izzy slunk back in his chair, ducking his head in disappointment.

Immediately, Annie's frown was transformed into a dazzling smile, and she passed me bowl after bowl of delicious food. It wasn't long before we were all talking and laughing. Izzy's antics and Gabriel's wild stories had their mother in fits from time to time. As she wiped her eyes with a corner of her napkin, I could tell that she was brimming with pride. Her boys were her life, and they fulfilled her. She lived for these Sundays and time with her family, and I felt blessed to be a witness to so much love and joy.

After the meal, I helped Gabe and Izzy do the dishes, against Annie's protests. She finally agreed to go and rest on the front porch swing with her mother and left the three of us alone in the kitchen. Gabe and Izzy teased and wrestled with each other. I washed, Izzy dried, and Gabe put the dishes away. I felt young again. Younger than I had in years. I wished that I could stay here always. I felt so warm and protected every time I was with Gabriel, and it was never suffocating. I knew that he loved me only for myself and not for what I could do for him.

When the afternoon finally drew to a close I was saddened to hear the approaching roar of Gabe's cousin in the old truck. He honked the horn a couple of times to let us know he was out front waiting. I gave Izzy a long hug goodbye and another to Gabe's grandmother. Finally I embraced Annie.

"Thank you so much, Mrs. Annie," I said.

She held me close to her and kissed my head.

"You are just so welcome!" she said, "Any time." I could see tears welling up in her eyes and suddenly I felt the urge to cry too.

"The Lord is with thee," she whispered in my ear. I pulled away and stared at her, surprised to see the knowing glint in her eyes. The next moment, Gabe had circled his arm around me, and was pulling me toward the door.

All the way back to the Palmers' house I thought about what Annie had said. I closed my eyes and leaned my head against Gabriel, knowing that it would be a long time before I could be with him again. He leaned over and kissed my cheek softly.

It had been one of the best days of my life.

CHAPTER SEVENTEEN

It was Good Friday, and I was alone, cleaning up the store. Bordelon had closed up at three o'clock as he did every year. After doing the receipts in his office, he locked the door and came out to put on his coat and hat. It was raining outside, a heavy April shower that soaked the streets and ran in tiny rivers down the windows.

"I'm gonna head out now," he said. "I gotta go home and change and then go pick up Sally."

Sally's parents were driving her to church that evening. It would be a long service. The priest would lead the faithful through the Stations of the Cross. I dreaded it and wished that I could somehow excuse myself, but I knew that I would be expected to join them.

"Sounds good, sir," I answered. "I'll see you at the church in a little while."

Bordelon grunted in reply. "Lock up and turn out the lights when you leave," he said over his shoulder.

"Always do." I answered.

I took my time sweeping the floor, restocking some of the shelves and wiping down the lunch counter. I could hear the church bell clanging mournfully and knew that the entire town would be deserted soon, everyone taking their places in their respective pews.

I was closing the blinds in the front window when I heard a loud pounding at the back door.   I couldn't imagine who it would be. Bordelon had a key, of course, and any customers would have come to the front. I marched quickly to the back and swung the door open.

It was Izzy Johnson. I had not seen him in weeks, and I was surprised at his sudden appearance.

"Izzy!" I shouted. "What brings you here?"

The little boy stared at me with wide eyes. Tears streaked his face and his clothes and hair were soaked with rain. I realized from the way that he was panting that he must have been riding his bicycle fast. His pants and shoes were covered with mud.

"Mr. Bram, please," he begged, "you gotta help us!"

"Sure, sure," I answered. "Come inside a minute and I'll get my things."

I held the door open and he came inside, shivering from the wet and peering anxiously around.

"Hurry, please, Mr. Bram," he urged.

I ran to the front of the store and made sure the door was locked, then returned to the back to grab my coat, hat and car keys. I flipped off the lights and then hurried back to Izzy.

"What's this about, Izzy?" I asked.

"It's my momma, Mr. Bram. She's in trouble. Please, you gotta come quick."

I opened the door and ushered him out, turned and locked the door behind me, and then grabbed his bicycle that was parked against the wall.

"Get in my car." I ordered. He quickly obeyed, and I threw open the trunk and tossed his bike inside.

I slid in behind the steering wheel, started up the car, and then pulled out of the parking lot, the car tires kicking up gravel and mud as I jerked the car into drive.

I glanced at Izzy who was sitting small and frightened in the passenger seat. His little face puckered and tears rolled down his cheeks.

"It's my fault!" he cried. "It's all my fault."

"Izzy don't say that!" I pleaded. "How can you say that? You can't help what your daddy's done."

"No, Mr. Bram, you don't understand," he mumbled. "It is my fault. None of this would have happened if it weren't for me."

He was right, I did not understand.

"What do you mean?" I asked.

He paused for a moment, trying to decide whether or not to tell me.

"Izzy, if you expect me to help you and your momma, you're gonna have to tell me the truth, now. What is going on?"

Izzy sighed and stared out the window.

"Do you remember back when someone took that necklace from Meyer's store?" he whispered.

"Yeah, yeah, I remember, why?"

"Well, I took it."

I sat silently for a moment. Izzy was still staring out the window, his hands clenched together in his lap.

"You took it? The Saint Anne necklace? How could you have taken it, Izzy? I heard what Warren Blanchard said about it. He said someone went through the side window. That's way up higher than you could reach, Izzy. Don't you mean your daddy took it?"

Izzy glared at me defiantly, wiping the tears from his cheeks.

"No sir, I mean I took it! I used my bike, and I stood up on the seat and I crawled my way inside."

I did not know how to respond to this.

"Why, Izzy? Why did you take that necklace?"

Izzy started crying again, putting his heads in his hands.

"I know it was wrong, Mr. Bram, but it was so pretty. It was so pretty and it had my momma's name on it, and I saw it in the window, and I just wanted to give it to her for her birthday." His words spilled out between sobs.

"Okay, okay," I said, "so you took it. That was wrong, Izzy, but you can give it back. We can make this right, can't we boy?"

"No, Mr. Bram," he sniffed, shaking his head at me, "it's too late, and now he's hurting my momma."

"Who's hurting your momma?" I asked, bewildered.

Izzy searched my face for a long moment, and then collapsed into sobs.

"Sheriff Boyle!" he wailed.

I was stunned. This was not at all the answer I expected. I waited a few moments for Izzy to recover himself and continue.

"He found out about it. He found out that I took that necklace and that my momma had it. He came to my house, and he said he was gonna take me and put me in jail and that my momma was never gonna see me again. So she begged and begged him not to, and that she'd do anything."

A growing feeling of dread began to gnaw the pit of my stomach. I pushed my foot down on the gas pedal, urging my car forward. How could I not have seen this?

"The sheriff started coming over to my house every night. He would pick up my momma from work and bring her home, and then he wouldn't leave. She would send me to my room and tell me not to come out. He would lock Gabriel out of the house. Sometimes he'd be drinking, and when he was drinking, he'd beat on her, and if I didn't go away fast enough he'd beat on me too."

I nodded and my mind raced back to the months before this: the time I had seen Annie in the store, and then Izzy. The strange way Gabe had acted when I asked him about his father. Vernon Johnson hadn't been the devil all along. It had been Sheriff Boyle!

"He's there right now, Mr. Bram," Izzy continued. "Miss Peg let my momma go home early today, on account of the holiday and the sheriff came over this afternoon. He's been drinking and he's been beating up on my momma! I ran out the back door to find Gabe, but I can't find him anywhere! So I came to the store to get you. Oh please, hurry, Mr. Bram. I think he's gonna kill her this time!"

I was getting closer to Izzy's house and was driving as fast as I could on the sloppy, muddy road. A few times my tires got stuck in a pot hole and spun out, and I had to throw my car into reverse, and then drive around the hole. Izzy was getting more and more frantic as time dragged on.

Finally we reached Annie Johnson's tiny house. The sheriff's cruiser was not there, and so I guessed that he had left. As soon as we pulled up, Izzy leaped out of the car and ran inside. I followed close behind, my heart pounding in my ears. I had no idea what I would find in that house.

"Momma, momma!" I heard Izzy screaming. I followed his voice and found myself in a tiny kitchen.

There was blood on the walls and smashed glasses and plates everywhere. Curled up in a heap in the corner of the room was Annie, her dress pulled up around her waist and the buttons open, revealing her brassiere. I barely recognized her, her face was so swollen and bloodied. Izzy was kneeling next to her, his arms wrapped around her shoulders, sobbing.

"Annie?" I whispered. "Oh my God, Annie. What happened? Did the sheriff do this?"

I already knew the answer.

Annie gazed up at me as if in a dream. Her eyes were almost swollen shut, but she slowly reached a hand up toward me.

I kneeled down beside her, pulling out my handkerchief and trying to gently wipe some of the blood from her lips. Her mouth was full of it, and she choked a bit as she tried to speak.

"Gabriel," she whispered.

"What's that, Annie? Was Gabriel here too?"

She nodded. "You have to find Gabe. You have to find my boy! He came home and he found the sheriff on me, and then he hit him! Hit him so hard he knocked him down. Then they fought, and Gabe hit him some more and knocked him out! I got scared. I told Gabe to run away, to run away and not come back! I told him to go to his cousin's house, and get him to take him to Baton Rouge to my sister's. So he left, and then after he left, the sheriff woke up and said he was going after him. I tried to stop him, Mr. Bram. I tried to stop him, but he just hit me again. He said he was going to find my boy, and when he found him he was gonna kill him!" at this she began to wail.

"You have to stop him, Mr. Bram!" she cried, clinging to my shirt and pulling my face close to hers. "You have to stop him! I can't lose my boy, Mr. Bram, I just can't!"

She pressed her face against my chest and sobbed, soaking my shirt with blood.

"It's alright Annie," I tried to reassure her. "It's alright. I'm gonna find the sheriff. I won't let him hurt your boy, I promise."

Izzy followed me out to the car. I pulled his bike out of the trunk and handed it to him.

"Go get some help, Izzy. Go get somebody to help your mother, and then stay here at the house, you here? I'm going to go try to find that son of a bitch sheriff and stop him."

Izzy nodded, jumped on his bike and pedaled away.

For the second time that day, I was pushing my car as fast as possible down the muddy gravel road that led from the Bottoms to town. The rain was pounding down harder now, making it even more difficult to drive. The slow pace was maddening to me, and as I drove I tried to come up with a plan for how I would handle a drunk and angry Boyle if it came to that. I decided that I should prepare myself for the worst, and so I turned the car toward my house to get my gun.

It had been years since I fired the revolver. I had bought it when I lived in New Orleans as protection on the streets. I kept it after I married Sally, although I never used it except for the occasional target practice. The truth was that the sound of a gunshot still unnerved me, even thirteen years after the war.

As I drove through the middle of town, I was struck by how deserted it was and then remembered that everyone was at church. It was now after six o'clock, and the sun was going down, although the rain clouds made the sky seem even darker. I knew that the service would be in full swing and would most likely not end until nearly eight.

I pulled into the driveway and drove around the house, slammed the car into park and then jogged across the yard to the back porch. As I entered the kitchen, I noticed all the lights were out. The bedroom door was open, and yet all was still and empty. I walked to the bedroom and peered inside. Dresser drawers were open and clothes were spilling out on the floor. There was a general disarray and silence, as though something terrible had happened.

Where was Melee? Sally must have gone to church with her parents. Did Melee run away? I went back to the kitchen and switched the light on, and then slowly made my way up the stairs.

The sun had gone down and the attic was quite dark. I switched on the light bulb and then began to rummage through the piles of books, furniture, and boxes, looking for the small metal case where I stored my gun. Minutes passed, and I began to get frustrated, thinking that the sheriff could have found Gabriel by now. I was about to give up when my foot hit something hard and I heard a metallic clang ring through the rafters. I picked up the box and then cursed. It was locked, of course, and I did not have the key with me.

I ran back downstairs to the kitchen and began frantically pulling out drawers and rifling through the contents. Finally I pulled open the silverware drawer and lifted the tray out. I stuck my hand in and reached all the way to the back. My fingers touched something small and cold. I pulled the key out and sighed in relief. Then I ran back upstairs to open the box.

I had pulled out the gun, loaded three bullets in and put it back together. I stood up and started to stuff the gun into my pants, then thought better of it and placed it back in the box. I hoped that I would not need to use it, and so I thought it would be best to just put the box in my glove compartment and only pull it out just in case.

As I turned to leave, a small noise stopped me. It was the sound of humming softly and it was coming from the spare bedroom. I noticed for the first time that the door was closed. There was no light coming from beneath it, so I assumed that Melee must be there, sitting in the dark. I could not understand why she would be there. It had been months since she had used that room. Sally had practically forbidden it, insisting that Melee stay in the bedroom. I had been using the spare room instead and because of that, Melee did not even come up to the garconniere at all anymore.

I walked over to the door to investigate. I knew that she would most likely not be happy to see me, but I decided that I should at least check to see if she was alright. As I got closer to the door, the humming got louder. It seemed to be some kind of lullaby although it was disjointed and strange. The melody was nothing that I recognized, but perhaps Melee was singing another one of the Cajun songs she had been taught as a child.

I put my hand on the door handle and slowly turned it. The door opened with a creak. It was dark outside and it was difficult to see in the room. Melee was seated on the bed with her back to me, humming and rocking gently.

"Melee?" I whispered. "Melee, are you alright?"

She stopped humming for a moment, completely still. I knew she had heard me, but she didn't turn around. Then a strangely familiar voice spoke.

"Bram, come inside, I have something wonderful to show you."

It was not Melee. It was Sally. Her voice was soft and low. She did not turn around, but began humming and rocking again.

"Sally?" I whispered again. "What are you doing here? Why didn't you go to church?"

I walked around the bed to the tiny table and turned on the light. What I saw next was something out of a nightmare.

The bed was in disarray. The sheets were tangled up and there was a strange odor in the room. It was an odor that I knew, but I had not smelled in a long time. It was the smell of blood.

The sheets were soaked in it. It was as though someone had been murdered in the bed. My eyes grew wide in horror. I felt a wave of nausea lurch up from my stomach to the back of my throat. I fought back the desire to vomit.

"Sally!" I choked. "What happened here?"

"Something wonderful," was the whispered reply.

She was seated at the foot of the bed, and for the first time I noticed that she was holding a bundle in her arms.

She turned her head toward me, her face held a vacant expression and her eyes were unfocused. The same expression my mother's had on that bus ride to Atlanta so long ago. And then I saw it – wrapped up in her arms in a bundle of bloody sheets, a tiny newborn baby. It wasn't moving. Its little head flopped unnaturally against Sally's shoulder. I realized that the poor little thing was dead.

"Isn't she beautiful?" Sally cooed, holding the lifeless child out toward me, limp as a ragdoll.

I threw myself backward against the table, covering my mouth. The baby was the color of caramel. Its head was covered by a shock of curly black hair. I knew it could not be mine.

"Oh my God, Sally. Where is Melee?" I tried to quell the panic that was racing through my blood.

"She's gone, Bram. That Gabriel came and got her," she murmured, smiling up at me. Then she turned back to the baby in her arms.

"Shh, shh, don't cry," she whispered, holding it close, "I'm your momma now, little one. I'm your momma now."

She started humming that strange tune again, and this time I recognized it:

In the sweet, by and by, we shall meet on that beautiful shore. . .

I was torn between helping Sally and going after Melee. I could not imagine how far they would have gotten on foot, or on Gabriel's bike.

"Oh, and Sheriff Boyle was here," Sally added. "Yes, he came right after they left. I think that he was looking for someone."

With that, I left her. I was running back down the stairs through the kitchen, and out to my car, clutching the metal strong box to my side. I only hoped that I wasn't too late.

CHAPTER EIGHTEEN

By the time I got back to my car it was seven o'clock. The rain was coming down even harder. As I fired up the engine again, I saw the windshield was completely fogged up. I took out my handkerchief and wiped down the inside. The quick pace of the wipers made a steady thumping noise that echoed the beating of my heart.

The pounding rain and fog that clouded the windows made it nearly impossible to see more than a few yards in front of the car. I went as fast as I could, the car's tires splashing through rivers of mud. I did not know which direction to head, so I decided to go back toward town. I wondered how far Melee and Gabriel had made it, and whether or not they had escaped Boyle.

I did a tour of the town square again, peering up and down streets and straining my eyes for any sign of the sheriff's cruiser. All was still deserted, the majority of the town's population still gathered inside the church. I could see the service in my mind: the faithful following the priest as he walked from station to station, singing O Sacred Head Surrounded.

Finally after nearly a half hour of searching, I parked my car in front of Meyer's store and turned off the ignition. The store was deserted, of course. Ira had closed up hours ago, going home to his wife, most likely to enjoy a quiet evening at home. I admired him. He was honest and genuine. When Ira was your friend, he was simply that – your friend. He was excluded from participating in Techeville's provincial attempt at high society, and so he did not operate from a desire to move in its circles. I regretted that I had not made an effort to get to know him better.

I sat thinking about the day, months before, when I had driven here after Blanchard and Boyle had taken Melee away. It seemed so long ago now, and yet it had not even been a year. Could all of this have happened in so short a time? I thought about that day – the fear I felt that I would be too late and the panic that Melee would be taken away from me. The way her face appeared when I went inside – so dejected and alone. I thought about leaving the store with her and how I had not known where to go, and had driven around aimlessly, searching for anywhere until I had pointed my car East.

Suddenly, it hit me: the only place where a colored boy and a white girl could blend in together without much notice, the same city I had gone to fresh out of the army, when I wanted to forget who I was and be forgotten. I started up my car again and headed out of town toward the bridge that would take me over Bayou Teche, out into the wild wetlands and straight toward New Orleans.

The road to the bridge was pitch black. Again, I moved along slowly, weaving my way around muddy potholes and sloshing through pools of water. As I neared the bridge, I noticed a light coming from it. It was the beam of headlights from a car parked there. I pulled up behind it. The taillights had an eerie glow in the fog. I thought perhaps someone had had trouble, and was waiting for help. There would not have been anyone driving over that bridge for hours – not with the whole town attending church.

I turned off my car's ignition, leaving my headlights on, and stepped out of the car. A familiar voice greeted me. The sound of it made my stomach lurch.

"Good evenin' Palmer," Boyle hooted, walking around from the side of his cruiser. He was holding a small flask in his hand, and he took a long swig as he sat down on the trunk of his car. When he had finished, he wiped his mouth with the back of his hand and threw the flask off the bridge into the raging water below.

"Some night to be driving around, eh Palmer?" Boyle chuckled then, folding his arms across his chest and staring menacingly at me.

"Boyle," I stammered, "I know what you've done. The game is up."

Boyle laughed at me, a low rumbling chuckle that built until it was booming across the bridge.

"Oh, the game is up, is it?" he sneered. "And what kind of game do you think I'm playin' there, Palmer?" He staggered a little on his feet, and steadied himself against the car. He was obviously drunk.

"I know that you've been blackmailing Annie Johnson. I know that you threatened to take Izzy away from her and you've been treating her like some kind of, of whore."

Boyle inspected me out of the corner of his eye and shook his head.

"Mmm, hmm. Well now, don't that beat all, eh Palmer? And what would you know about whores? Oh wait, I think you know a lot about whores, don't you, Palmer?"

He took a step toward me, and I backed away, wishing I had taken that damn gun out of the strong box and put it in my pocket.

"What are you talking about?" I asked.

"Come on, now, Palmer. What, you think you've got everybody fooled about that coon-ass bitch you been keeping at your house? It's damn near disgusting what you've been doing over at your place!" He laughed again.

I was beginning to feel panicky, my breath quickening, and my heart beating loudly in my ears.

"What the hell are you talking about?" I demanded, hoping to call his bluff.

"Oh, come off it Palmer. I've been casing your place since last Fall. Blanchard had me watching you. He was pretty pissed off that that bitch got out of stealing that necklace. He was hoping I might see something that would prove otherwise." He put his hand on his chest and let out a long burp.

"Well, I saw a whole hell of a lot more than that, Palmer!" he hooted, "Lordy, the things I saw at your house! Course, I found the necklace eventually on Annie Johnson, so I wasn't hunting for that anymore, but I have to tell you Palmer, I started coming over to watch just from the sheer fun of it."

I shuddered, thinking about what Melee had said about "the devil" watching her, and the black figure I had seen from the window that night. It had been Boyle all along.

"So it was you," I mumbled.

"Hell, yeah, it was me. What, did you think it was Vernon Johnson? That would be a ghost, now wouldn't it?"

"I, I don't, what do you mean?" I stammered.

Boyle laughed again, clearly enjoying himself. "I guess I can tell you Palmer. It don't make too much difference anymore. Vernon Johnson's dead. I didn't just run em out of town, Palmer. When I do a job, I do it all the way, you see."

He saw my confusion, and snickered at me.

"I killed him, Palmer. I drug that nigger behind my cruiser a few miles, and then I threw him over this here bridge! Blanchard didn't like that too much, though. He nearly cut me off after that." With that, he spat on the ground, his face growing angry.

"Well he can go straight to hell! I don't know who that hypocrite thinks he is, anyhow, with his fancy cars and his high fallutin' ways. That son of a bitch wouldn't of had any of it if it weren't for me! You think he'd won nearly as many cases if I weren't there helping him?"

Boyle's voice was getting louder and more aggressive. I took another step backwards.

"No! He wouldn't have. But do you think he ever thanked me? Hell no! Instead he gave me a lecture. Told me I needed to cool it. Said I needed to watch myself. 'Just can't have the same kind of justice around here like we used to.'"

He stared off into space, clearly thinking of something for a moment. Then he turned a glare back on me.

"I didn't tell him about Annie, though. No, I kept that one just for me! Figure she owed it to me anyhow, seeing as how I took care of her husband," he started chuckling again.

A shock of rage ripped through me as I remembered how Annie had been earlier, lying bloodied and helpless on her kitchen floor.

"Yeah, I've seen how you took care of Annie," I hissed. "You're no better than Vernon was!"

"Well now, Palmer, that ain't too gentlemanly of you, now is it?" he sneered. "But then, you wouldn't know much about being a gentleman. You're only one rung up above poor white trash as far as I can see. I guess you couldn't keep up that charade for too long, though. You sure did enjoy that little Cajun hussy for a while, now didn't you?"

I clenched my fists, anger boiling up behind my eyes.

"Don't try to deny it, Palmer," he sneered. "I seen all of it. You ain't too discreet, I have to say. But I also seen it didn't last too long. Guess she got tired of you quick."

I tried to make sense of what he was saying and opened my mouth to speak.

"Shoo eee, Palmer! You look like a damn catfish standing there with your mouth opening and closing," he snorted. "Guess you didn't make too fine of a lover, did you? You must have been pretty awful, seeing as how she dropped you and went on to your lawn boy."

"My . . .Gabriel? What do you mean?"

"Oh, come on, now Palmer, you mean you don't know?" he waited for a moment, and when he saw my bewilderment, bent over shrieking in laughter.

"Yeah, Gabriel Johnson!" he managed to get out between gasps. "I seen 'em together one day, in your garage of all places, Palmer! It was so sweet, and all, them two lying together on an old drop cloth in the corner. Must've been Gabe's first time, too."

"But you, if you knew, why didn't you. . ."

"Why didn't I do something about it? No need, Palmer! You see, I figured Gabriel was the last piece of the puzzle. I got awful tired of him interfering with me and Annie, you know, he'd come home and see me there and make a fuss. Well, after I saw him on that Cajun girl, we just came to a little gentlemanly agreement. He would keep his mouth shut about his momma and me, and I'd just pretend like I didn't see nothing either."

I shook my head, hoping that by doing so I could shake out the words that he was saying to me, but I knew that they were true. I thought again about the little mulatto baby in Sally's arms.

"It was all fine and good until tonight," Boyle continued. "Then I guess Gabe forgot our agreement." He rubbed his jaw, and for the first time I saw that his face was swollen and he was getting what looked like a black eye.

"I don't take too kindly to being hit by stupid colored boys." He said. "That son of a bitch crossed a line. He knew what he done, too. That's why he ran away, but it didn't take me too long to find him. I figured he'd be running back to get his lady love, and when I went to your house and saw that they were both gone, I came after them. They got all the way to the bridge, too. Dumb shit didn't even have a car. That Cajun girl was riding on the handle bars of his bike."

With that, Boyle walked over and began pulling a mangled bicycle from beneath the back fender of his cruiser.

"Hey, Palmer, wanna give me a hand here? This bike's done a number on my car."

I recoiled again, in horror. The realization of what had happened was slowly entering my brain.

Boyle glanced up at me and then sighed in disgust, "Oh come on now, you don't really CARE about those two do you? I mean it's just a nigger boy and a coon-ass girl. Two pieces of trash that needed to be cleaned off the street as far as I'm concerned."

"What did you do?" I whispered, unable to find my voice.

"What did I do?" Boyle hooted again, turning toward me. "Well, ain't it obvious Palmer? I stopped the son of a bitch! He put up a good fight, but he didn't say too much once he was under my car." He chuckled again, enjoying the joke he'd made.

"Threw him over the bridge just like his daddy. And good riddance! Last thing we need is another no-good nigger in this world."

I looked over the side of the bridge, tears beginning to well up in my eyes. I thought about Gabe's laughing face. All the dreams that he had to make a better life for himself and his mother. How smart and kind he was.

"Wh – what about the girl?" I stammered.

"Oh now, that was sad, that was," he said, sarcasm lacing his voice. "She was screaming and all, after her lover boy went over the side. Talking that Cajun gibberish they speak. I didn't want her carrying on like that, so I offered to drive her somewhere. Hell, wherever those swamp rats live, you never can tell. She just stared at me, you know, crying."

He gazed out into space again, remembering what had happened.

"Well then, she did the damnedest thing, Palmer. She got up on the side of the bridge, and she jumped after him!"

The weight of what he said slammed into me like a freight train. It knocked the breath out of me. I bent over and grabbed my knees, sucking in deep breaths of air, fighting back my urge to vomit.

"Hey, you alright, there Palmer?" Boyle asked. "Ah, what the hell. There's plenty more cheap Cajun pussy where she came from."

Boyle shook his head again, then shrugged his shoulders and turned back to his car and started trying to pull the bicycle out from under it again. I started to shake from head to toe with rage. I struggled to pull myself upright, and then stalked back toward my car, pulling open the door and leaning over to the passenger seat.

My mind filled with a vision of Melee sitting there the first night I'd brought her home, soaking wet, water pouring off her hair, her tiny hands clasped white and frail in her lap. She turned toward me as if to speak, opened her mouth and black water spilled from it. I cried out in fear and shut my eyes. When I opened them, the vision had vanished. I leaned across the seat and opened the glove compartment, pulling out the metal strong box.

I sat back up with the strong box on my lap and stared out through my windshield. The rain was still pouring down, and the headlights cut through the fog, shining on Boyle as he dragged Gabriel's mutilated bicycle over to the side of the bridge. I fumbled with the gun, checking again that it was loaded, feeling its icy cold weight in my hands. Boyle was lifting the bike up to the side, I could see his neck muscles flexing with the strain. I slipped out of my car again, holding the gun out in front of me and walking toward him.

"Oh, there you are, Palmer," he panted, "Give me a hand, would ya?" He glanced over at me and saw the gun in my hand. Confusion spread across his face for a moment, and then he broke out into peals of laughter.

"Hoo hoo! Palmer, you are a funny son of a bitch, ain't ya? What the hell do you think you're doing there? You're not in the army anymore."

I shuddered for a moment, fighting through my fear. I hated him for how weak I felt.

"Boyle, I've done a lot of things I regret in my life, but killing you will not be one of them."

"Kill me? Please, Palmer, pull the other one." He let go of the bike, which was perched on the ledge of the bridge and took a step backward. I walked closer to him, pointing the gun directly in his face.

"Just a minute, now Palmer. Calm down. Damn, boy you are as nervous as a school girl!" He leaned against the side for a moment, squinting up at me.

"Go to hell!" I snapped, but still wasn't able to pull the trigger.

"Alright, fine then, Palmer. Kill me. I guess you got reason enough to. Guess you can make up whatever kind of story you like about it. Course, you'll probably end up in Angola before the year's out, but that ought not to bother you, right Palmer? I mean, you know what prison's like, don't you?"

I wavered for a moment, the thought of prison filled me with terror and dread. I knew that I would have to kill myself before that happened. Boyle saw my hesitation and continued.

"OR," he said, "you and I can make a little agreement here. You ain't gonna say nothing, and I ain't gonna. What happened here was a sad little tragedy. Two young lovers got swept off the bridge on a rickety ol' bike. Won't be too many folks searching for them anyway. Then I'll go back to my house and you go back to yours."

I shook my head and took another step forward, "No deal."

"Come on now, Palmer, let's think this through here. Hell, I promise I won't touch Annie Johnson again if it'll make you feel better, and you know I won't tell anybody about that little dead bastard baby back at your place."

I froze instantly. This was not something that I had counted on. Boyle took another step toward me, growing in confidence.

"See, I think you might be able to come out of this real nicely, there Palmer. You need to go home and do a little clean up of course. Get rid of that baby and make up some story for Sally. Hell, that girl's mind is gone anyhow. Eventually she'll get over it, and if she don't, well, you'll have her put in a nice asylum and have that place and all her inheritance to yourself."

I stood wavering for a moment, and then dropped my arm, grief overwhelming me. I sank to my knees, disgusted at all I had done, through my action and inaction and at my inability to make any of it right. I dropped the gun and clamped my arms against my stomach. A second later I felt Boyle next to me. He picked up the gun and chucked it into the Bayou. Then he shoved Gabe's bike over the side and wiped his hands on his pants.

"Go home, Palmer," mumbled Boyle. "Hurry up. They'll all be out of church soon." The sheriff got into his cruiser and drove away.

CHAPTER NINETEEN

Today was my birthday. I didn't tell anyone, but when I woke up this morning, I lay for a moment, thinking about it. Bram was already gone to work, and I heard Sally rummaging around in the kitchen, making something for me to eat. At any moment she would come back into the bedroom and force something into me. I relished the brief moments like these when I could just be alone and think.

I was looking forward to the evening. Sally and Bram would be gone to the Good Friday services for hours, and Gabriel had promised to come and get me. He said he had a surprise for me, but he promised that we would do something fun for my birthday. It would be another brief moment of joy and excitement for me in what had been months of dull monotony.

It was a cloudy morning. I could tell by the way the light in the room was muffled. Marraine always called me her 'tite ouaouaron' – little frog – because I was born in the middle of a rainstorm. Most of my birthdays had been rainy days.

I thought for a moment about my own little frog, the one who danced and hopped and kicked inside me. I put my hand on my belly and waited for him. Normally he woke me up with his antics, but this morning he had been still and quiet. Too quiet.

"Morning, sunshine!" Sally crooned, bursting into the room with a serving tray. "How are we this morning?"

She placed the tray on the bedside table and handed me a cup of orange juice. I sat up slowly in bed and took a sip of the juice. Sally busied herself about the room, opening the curtains and pulling out fresh clothes for me to wear.

After I had nibbled an acceptable amount I got up and, taking the dress that Sally had laid out for me, headed to the bathroom. Sally had drawn a bath for me and I pulled off my nightgown and stepped inside. The water was warm and soothing. I slipped down under the surface, just the top of my huge belly remaining out of the water. I sat very still, holding my breath, hearing nothing under the water except for the sound of my own heart.

The pain started as an ache in my lower back. I sat up slowly, placing my hands on my stomach and bending forward. The next moment, the pain was shooting up my spine and radiating into my lower abdomen. I felt my stomach harden, and I pulled my knees up, trying to stifle the gasps that racked through me. Gripping the side of the tub, I tried to stand up, but the pain pushed me back again.

"Everything alright in there?" I heard Sally calling.

"Y- yes ma'am," I choked out. I knew I only had a few more moments before she would be knocking at the door.

I struggled again to stand up, and as I did, another wave of pain ripped through me. I cried out in earnest this time. I looked down and saw blood flowing from me, down my legs, staining the water with cloudy red. The next instant, Sally had thrown the door open, shock and horror on her face.

"Oh, Jesus!" she screamed. "Oh no, Lord, Jesus!" She ran over to me, grabbing me under the arms and helping me to step out of the tub.

"I, I'm sorry. ." I stammered.

"Shh, shh, now, don't speak," she soothed, wrapping a towel around me. "Can you walk?" she asked.

"I think so."

I leaned my head against Sally's shoulder and together we limped toward the bedroom. When I reached the foot of the bed, another wave of pain shot through me and I toppled forward, gripping the quilt in my hands.

"Oh my God!" Sally yelled. "Melee, can you get into the bed, honey? Oh God, Oh God." She was panting in her effort to lift me up. I managed to help her pull me up and then rolled into the bed.

The next few hours passed in a blur. I drifted in and out of consciousness, moving from blinding pain, to frightening dreams. At one point, I sat up in bed, screaming,

"Marraine! Viens! Marraine! J'ai besoin de toi!"

Sally was next to me, shushing me and rubbing a cool cloth across my forehead.

"Miss Sally," I whispered, settling back against the pillow. "You have to call someone. Please, call a doctor."

Sally pursed her lips and shook her head. "I can't honey, now you know that. No one can see you have this baby, you understand, don't you, sugar?"

"Miss Sally, I'm so sorry. I don't think the baby made it."

"Don't say that!" she snapped. "I won't hear that. You will not say that again!" She got up suddenly and left the room, slamming the door.

I was alone for another hour, tossing and turning. I felt as though I was burning alive. My sweat soaked the sheets. Sally finally returned and gasped when she saw me.

"Oh God, honey," she said. "I'm sorry I left. I had to go and get some things."

She was holding a bowl with some linens, scissors, string and various other supplies. I tried to sit up again and when I did saw that I was lying in blood. Blood soaked the sheets and the quilts.

Sally seemed to notice it, and muttered,

"Got to get you up out of here, now. My parents are coming, and I can't have you in here like this. Got to get you upstairs."

She put her arms around me and started to drag me out of the bed. The pain was excruciating now. I gasped with each step. Sally's jaw was clenched, and she held me in an iron grip as she half pulled, half dragged me out of the bedroom, across the kitchen, up the stairs, through the attic, and finally into the small bedroom where I had stayed when I first came to live at the Palmers.

By the time we reached it, I was crying in pain. Sally threw me on the bed, and pulled me backward. She had laced sheets through the head of the bed, and she placed my hands in them, threading them around my wrists like handcuffs. I saw by the expression on her face that she no longer had any concern for my welfare. Her only concern was for the baby inside me.

After she had tied me down, she placed a gag into my mouth and then stroked my cheek.

"Shh, shh," she whispered, "try not to cry out so, ok honey? My parents are coming in a minute to get me for church. I need to go downstairs and clean up a little and tell them that I'm not feeling well – that I've got a headache and they need to go without me. Now, you just try to be quiet, and I'll be back as quick as I can."

She kissed me on the cheek. Then she took one last peek around the room, closed and locked the door.

I bit down on the wadded cloth in my mouth and allowed myself to scream, grateful for the way the sound was muffled. I thought about Marraine, the many times that I had been with her when she went to aid the women in labor. There had been pain, of course, but Marraine had soothed them, bringing them tonics and teas to ease the pain, rubbing their backs, massaging them, singing to them. They called her an angel, and she was. I wanted so much to see her again, to feel her cool hand on my head and know that everything would be ok.

An hour or so later, Sally returned, a bowl of hot water in her arms. She was humming a strange tune. She barely looked at me.

"Are you ready to come out, my love?" she crooned to the unborn baby. "Momma's ready for you."

She kneeled at the foot of the bed and pulled out her rosary. Slowly and methodically, she began reciting the Our Father.

Our Father, who art in heaven,

"M-Miss S-Sally!" I gasped, "help me!"

Hallowed be thy name

"Please, Miss Sally, please, I don't know what to do!"

Thy kingdom come, thy will be done, on earth as it is in heaven,

"Miss Sally, I beg you, please get someone to help me!"

Give us this day our daily bread, and forgive us our trespasses,

I lost consciousness then. I became aware only of the pain. I felt myself screaming, though I made no sound. Somewhere in the distance, I could still hear Sally's voice.

For thine is the kingdom, the power, and the glory, now and forever, Amen.

Finally the pain subsided. I don't know how much time passed. I felt as though I were floating above the bed, and when I looked down, I saw myself there, leaning lifeless against the pillows, my legs askew and Sally kneeling at the foot of the bed, her rosary pressed against her lips which were moving rapidly in silent prayer.   I gradually came back to myself, and when I opened my eyes, Sally was rising to her feet, her rosary beads clutched in her hands, her eyes wide with wonder. I glanced down at my legs and saw pools of blood and there in between, a tiny shriveled baby. The baby was not moving. It was not making the cries that it should be making. It was too tiny to be born, I knew. It was not its time.

"It's a girl!" Sally squealed, picking up the tiny thing and wrapping it in a towel. She wiped the blood from its head and kissed it, then she began dancing from foot to foot, singing a song low and softly.

"Thank you, Melee," she said, her voice quiet and firm. "You can go now."

She turned her back to me and stared out the window. I had been ready for this. I'd known for a while that as soon as the baby was born, Sally would no longer need me, and I'd be free to go. I pulled myself together, weak and shivering. I tried to stand up, but swayed unsteadily on my feet. Where would I go now? There was still no answer for me. There still did not seem to be a place of safety and comfort waiting for me anywhere.

"Melee!" I heard a voice shouting from below. "Melee!"

It was Gabriel. My angel.

"Gabriel!" I called back. "I'm up here!"

I heard feet running through the kitchen, and then bounding up the kitchen stairs. In another moment he arrived at the door, his eyes bright. The smile faded from his lips, and I watched as he took in the scene, his eyes flitting from me, to the bed, to Sally and back to me. I held my arms out to him, and he bounded over to my side, pulling me close to him.

"Melee, you alright honey? What happened? What happened?"

"Please," I choked, "please, get me out of here."

Gabriel didn't answer. He picked me up in his strong arms and strode out of the room. He brought me downstairs and into the bathroom.

"Can you walk a little?" he asked, "Can I leave you here for a minute? I'm going to get your things together."

I nodded. I could feel the strength returning to me, now that the pain was gone. I washed off the blood as best as I could, and wrapped myself in a dry towel. Gabriel returned in a moment, bringing me clothes to put on. He already had my little carpet bagged packed up for me. I stumbled out of the bathroom, and he grabbed my hand.

"Melee, I have to leave. Now." I saw fear and anger in his eyes. "Honey, you don't have to go with me, but if you want to, you sure can."

I didn't answer. I just put my arms around his neck, pulling his lips to mine. We kissed for a long moment, and then he picked me up and carried me outside. He put me on the handlebars of his bike, placing my little bag in my lap and climbing on. The next minute we were pedaling on our way out of town.

The rain was pounding down. Soaking me through. I could barely see in front of us. Gabriel put his chin on my shoulder. I heard him gasping with the effort of pushing his bike through the mud and pools of rainwater. We rode that way for a long time, not speaking, nothing but the sound of the rain and Gabe's ragged breath in my ear. I was grateful that the entire town would be at church tonight. I was grateful for the rain and the darkness to cover us as we made our escape.

We reached the bridge over Bayou Teche, and Gabriel started the steep climb. We slowed down more and more and I could tell that Gabe was really struggling now to push the both of us up.

"Gabe," I said, "Let me walk!"

"No, Melee, it's ok, I can get us up there!"

"Gabe," I argued, "please, I can walk now. I'm ok. Really I am." He stopped the bike, and I climbed down. He gave me a grateful smile, and the two of us began walking slowly up and over the bridge.

I didn't hear the car coming. I guess the sound of the rain drowned it out. All I know is that we were almost to the middle of the bridge when suddenly we were both blinded by headlights. Gabriel stopped and turned around, his face angry and defiant. The car stopped, its headlights still shining on us and then someone stepped out of the driver's side.

I instantly recognized the silhouette. Though I could not see his face, I saw the dark shape of his body and knew it from a thousand nightmares both waking and asleep. It was the Vieux Diable. This time, though, he spoke.

"Evening, Gabriel. Well, now, where do you think you're going?"

"That – that ain't your business, Sheriff!" Gabriel shouted. He put out his arm and pushed me behind him.

"Well now, Gabe, I'm afraid you made it my business earlier this evening, didn't you?" The sheriff was slowly walking around the car door and heading toward us, his hand perched on his gun holster.

"And what have we here?" he continued, "a little companion to join you? How sweet."

"She ain't got nothin' to do with this!" said Gabriel.

"I say she has!" hissed the sheriff, "I just come from Sally Palmer's place and I seen what's been left there. I say she has a lot of explaining to do."

Gabriel threw a panicked look in my direction. "Run, Melee!" he urged me, "RUN!"

I didn't wait for him to say it again, I turned, grabbing my carpet bag and took off over the bridge. I thought that Gabriel was right behind me with the bicycle.

"GET BACK HERE!" I heard the sheriff scream, and then I heard the slam of a car door, the roar of an engine and the screech of tires peeling out on wet road. When I turned back to see if Gabriel were behind me, I saw the sheriff's cruiser slamming into the bicycle, and Gabriel's body was flung forward to the ground.

"NO!" I screamed, dropping my bag and running back to Gabriel. Blood was pouring from his head where it had smacked the pavement. He did not move, though I called and called him, my head buried in his chest. I felt something pushing me aside. I looked up and saw the sheriff bending over us. His face was hard and fierce. He picked Gabriel up off the ground and flung him over his shoulder. For an instant I thought the sheriff was going to help us, but then I watched as he walked carefully over to the side of the bridge and, without pausing, threw Gabriel's body over the ledge and into the Bayou Teche.

I felt a wave of despair and grief rip through me. I was sobbing and screaming as I ran over to the ledge to see if I could see Gabriel's body, but when I looked over there was nothing but the violent rush of black water below.

"Hush up now," said the sheriff. "Don't keep carrying on like that, you're giving me a headache! Hush up, I said!" he shouted, walking toward me.

But I couldn't stop screaming. I had stayed quiet for so long that to stop the flood of sadness that was coming out of me would be like trying to stop the raging waters of the Bayou Teche.

"Shut up!" he yelled. "Shut up! Listen, I'll take you home, you hear me? I'll take you anywhere you want to go, just stop that screaming, would you?"

He took another few steps toward me, reaching out his hand to grab my arm. At that instant I felt myself compelled forward by rage and fear. There was only one place I wanted to be now, and that was with Gabriel. I climbed up onto the ledge, and before the sheriff could stop me, I jumped off into the water below.

I don't know how long I stayed under water. I felt myself hurtling forward, spinning and tumbling in the raging current. I saw nothing and heard nothing but the sound of the water churning and rushing through my ears. Time passed: minutes, hours, days. An eternity passed. I felt the water slowing down. I was drifting now, cradled and rocked gently. I was floating on my back. The water was soothing and warm. I felt safe and protected. I felt as though I could open my eyes, and when I did, I saw a glow ahead of me, coming from the side of the river bank, and heard voices, kind voices singing to me.

The current slowed down even more, and I felt myself moving closer and closer to the light. I realized it was the glow of candles. I began to see them as separate orbs of lights and I counted them: one, two, three, four, five. I drew closer and closer to the candlelight, and the darkness began to drain away from around me. I began to make out the words of the song being sung to me from the riverbank:

In the sweet, by and by, we shall meet on that beautiful shore . . .

The next moment I had the sensation of strong arms lifting me up from the water. I opened my eyes and saw Gabriel's smiling face close to mine. He pulled me out of the water and set me on my feet on the river bank. He left me there, and turned to an old woman who was holding a little baby in her arms. She handed the baby to him, and he took the baby in one hand and a candle in the other. The little baby girl was holding a candle too. She smiled up at me, giggling, shaking her curly black hair. Her skin was the color of caramel, and her eyes were gray-green like mine.

I walked toward them for a moment, and my heart leapt at the sound of a voice that called me.

"Tite Melee?"

"Marraine!"

It was her, even more beautiful than I remembered her. She held a gnarled hand out to me and I put mine in hers. She was so strong and gentle.

"Hello, sweetheart," came another voice. It was my grandmother, her white halo of hair floating around her pretty wrinkled face. She took my other hand in hers, and I walked forward between the two pillars of my childhood. Each held a candle in one hand and pulled me along with the other. Gabriel and the baby girl followed along behind.

Ahead in the distance, there was one more candle. We didn't speak, but I knew that we were heading toward it with purpose. I felt excitement building in my chest, though I didn't know why. As we got closer I saw that the candle was held by a woman – beautiful and tall, with blond hair, but with the same gray-green eyes that I shared with the baby girl. She seemed not much older than me. I had never seen her before, and yet there was something so familiar about her. I wanted to run to her, to put my arms around her neck and hold her tightly.

She smiled at me, holding a lit candle in one hand and an unlit one in the other. As I approached, she held the wick of the one into the flame of the other, transferring the light over, and then she handed the brightly burning candle out to me.

"Amy Lee," she said. "I have been waiting a long time."

And with that, my mother laced her arm around my waist and led me away to eternity

THE END

ABOUT THE AUTHOR

Jackie Shemwell is a native of Louisiana with a degree in French and a love of Francophone Cajun folklore. She weaves personal experience and family history into her writing. She's also a wife to Wade and mom to Zach and Josh (and fur-baby Zoe). She's a daughter, a friend, and a lover of coffee, white wine (sadly, allergic to red) cheese, cooking (especially other people's) and travel.

Made in the USA
San Bernardino, CA
09 March 2016